DATE DUE

THE
FINAL
TALLY

*Also by Richard S. Wheeler
in Thorndike Large Print*

Winter Grass
Sam Hook
Stop
Incident at Fort Keogh
Fool's Coach
Montana Hitch
Where the River Runs

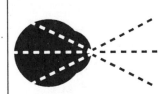

This Large Print Book carries the
Seal of Approval of N.A.V.H.

THE FINAL TALLY

Richard S. Wheeler

Thorndike Press • Thorndike, Maine

Library of Congress Cataloging in Publication Data:

Wheeler, Richard S.
   The final tally / Richard S. Wheeler.
      p.   cm.
   ISBN 1-56054-242-X (alk. paper : lg. print)
   1. Large type books. I. Title.
[PS3573.H4345F5   1992]   91-23420
813'.54—dc20   CIP

Thorndike Press Large Print edition published in 1992
by arrangement with Ballantine Books, a division of
Random House, Inc.

Cover design by Michael Anderson.

The tree indicium is a trademark of Thorndike Press.

This book is printed on acid-free, high opacity paper.

THE

FINAL

TALLY

Chapter 1

The Mexican at the door looked like he'd never been inside a day in his life. A blue-eyed Mexican, squinting at him from eyes too familiar with the sun. A drover obviously, wearing a dirty green bandanna; ancient, faded blue shirt; and battered chapaderos worn shiny by endless hours in the saddle.

"I'm looking for a doctor. They said — " The man's eyes spotted Santiago Toole's steel star, pinned on his black vest. "I'm sorry. I don't need a sheriff. . . ."

"I'm Dr. Toole."

"You're wearing a star."

"I'm both. I practice medicine whenever I'm called, and I'm sheriff of Custer County, too. You need help?"

"No, I don't feature it. Is there some other pillpopper in Miles City?"

"At Fort Keogh. Dr. Hoffmeister is the post surgeon there."

"An army sawbones?" The news seemed to disturb the man even more. Santiago Toole waited, sensing something unusual about this.

"If you need help, I'll come help," Toole said. "I'm here to help people every way I can."

"We're treed," the man admitted reluctantly. "Got some injured. And one sick."

"You're a drover with that herd coming down the Tongue River," Santiago said.

The man nodded. "Jefferson Gonzales. I'm the segundo. I put spurs on that bayo coyote *cabrón* I'm riding and came ahead. They should be three or four miles south of town when we get there."

"What sort of wounds? I need to know what to take."

"You'll see when you get there."

"If there's more than one injured, we can get Dr. Hoffmeister."

"No. You come, *compadre*. You'll do."

Santiago Toole sighed. He'd sort it out later. He raced back to the kitchen, where Mimi was preparing corned beef and cabbage, and told her he'd be out on call. Then he saddled his big bay thoroughbred gelding, tightening the latigo carefully because the bay had a way of holding its breath while being cinched, and trotted the horse around to the picket fence where Jefferson Gonzales waited on his gaunt dun pony. In one of Toole's saddlebags were his medical supplies and in the other sheriff things, including manacles and spare ammunition. He wished he'd had time to get out of his black britches and waistcoat and

8

white collarless shirt, but the man seemed to be in a hurry.

"Which bank of the Tongue?" he asked.

"The east."

Gonzales raked Toole's long, lean horse with knowing eyes and then swung away, bursting into an easy lope that spelled urgency and distance to Santiago. Ahead of him the old wiry drover flew through river brush and cottonwood groves, following an ancient trail along the bottoms of the Tongue River. Santiago spurred his big bay, less comfortable than the old Mexican but determined not to lag. The late afternoon light gilded the slow, September-dried river on his right and blazoned the eastern bluffs with gold.

Jefferson Gonzales. Probably an Anglo mother and Mexican father. That would explain the man's English, Toole thought. They continued to lope for another six or seven minutes, until they burst out of the brushy area surrounding the confluence of the Tongue and the Yellowstone rivers. Then the old man slowed to a swift walk. Santiago pulled up beside him on the wider trail, brimming with questions.

"Whose herd is it, Mr. Gonzales?"

The man squinted at him distrustfully. "Belongs to Bragg. Hermes Bragg, from down near San Antonio."

9

"That's a long way."

"Twice as far as the Kansas railroad, and we're not where we're going yet."

"You're the seventh herd from Texas this year," Toole said, finding Gonzales more relaxed when talking about cattle than about medicine.

"We're heading for the Judith country if we can make it before winter shuts us down."

"That's still a piece," said Santiago. "No one there except some buffalo."

Jefferson Gonzales nodded, as if that were a datum that had decided where this herd would go.

"How many head?"

Gonzales gave him that squinty look again. "Started with well over two thousand," he muttered. "I don't know how it tallies now."

"All common cattle?"

Gonzales was slow to answer. "Cimarrones, mostly. It gets harder to trail them all the time. Wire's up now. Quarantines. They don't like Texas beef none. They talk about this Texas fever killing other beef, but I don't see any of it."

Far up the Tongue River valley Santiago spotted yellow haze, possibly dust from the movement of a giant herd. "That them?" he asked.

Gonzales nodded.

"Who's the worst off? Who should I be seeing first?"

Gonzales spat. "Iturbide. Isodoro Iturbide. He's nearly cashiered."

"Fevers? Typhoid?"

"Gutshot."

Toole's mind raced. A sheriff matter, then. Maybe an army matter. And yet, if he read Gonzales right, the man wanted no part of the law or army.

"Better tell me the rest, Gonzales. How long ago? Who? Why?"

"Over a week ago. Two others hurt. One through the cheek. Blew out some jaw and teeth and got to mortifying. The other's got a hole in his thigh."

"And?"

"And the old man, Hermes Bragg, he's flat on his back with consumption. His children driving that wagon; the others we got in the cavvy wagon."

"You haven't told me what happened."

"Sioux."

The news startled Santiago. Hardly commonplace in 1881, although there'd been some renegades. Lots of those, young ones mostly, refusing to reconcile themselves to reservation life.

It occurred to him that Indians got blamed for things they didn't do — such as putting

11

bullets in three cowboys. Maybe there'd been a brawl among them, the pressures of the trail boiling over into blood. He said nothing though. The doctoring came first.

"It can happen," he said softly. "I hear they're mighty hungry."

He let it go at that, and they rode quietly southwest in a shallow trough cut into naked dun prairie. Gonzales volunteered nothing more either but kept glancing at Santiago with distrustful azure eyes. The man had secrets, large ones, and Santiago suspected he would find the identical attitude among the other drovers. None of them would be talking.

Ahead he saw a low wall of beef ambling northward in the low, late sun, stopping for nothing. Longhorns, mostly the black cimarrones, but every color of the rainbow as well, dun and copper and brindle. Red and brown and white and spotted. The lead animal walked relentlessly forward, slavering at the mouth slightly because of the late summer heat, its head bobbing and its giant horns, one hooked up and the other down, swinging like scythes. Two riders in white shirts and wide-brimmed hats rode point on tough little Texas cayuses showing mustang blood. And behind, lost in golden dust, came the body of the herd, lowing and bawling and shaking the hard clay of the Tongue valley with a strange, trembling thunder.

"Sick are at the rear in wagons, eating dust. Guess we'll ride around," Gonzales said shortly. He steered toward the bluffs and climbed halfway up the blistered flank of one before he cut southward. The spectacle stunned Santiago. For perhaps two miles — he couldn't be sure because of the golden dome of dust over the herd — beeves stretched backward, contained by pairs of flank riders ambling easily beside the living river of animals.

"This must be the largest herd to reach Montana Territory," said Santiago. "I've never seen the like."

Gonzales grunted and pushed ahead. Moments later they plunged into choking dust, driven eastward by gentle west winds. Day turned into dun dusk. Santiago's guide hoisted his bandanna over his face, looking like a bandit, but Santiago Toole had none and coughed his way forward, feeling the alkali saturate his clothing, begrime his neck, powder his britches. It rolled off his bay horse with every twitch of muscle as the animal reacted to dense black clouds of flies. Hell on earth, thought Santiago. Trailing herds was work to drive men mad with pain and heat and ceaseless toil. He followed the ghostlike form ahead of him grimly, grateful not to make his living trailing cattle from one end of a continent to the other.

Then the dust thinned, and Santiago made out the drag, half-a-dozen riders hazing laggards forward. They were bronze with dust: their hats, faces, bandannas, and every scrap of clothing they wore. Even at that they were lucky, he thought. They had a quartering wind. On any day heading into the wind the drag position would be pure hell.

"Over there," said Gonzales.

Three wagons, each drawn by a mule team. All of them well back of the herd to escape the dust. On days without crosswinds, they probably ranged well forward of the herd. Santiago recognized one bulky gray wagon, the chuck, a traveling commissary and kitchen. Another looked to be a small version of the immigrant wagons he'd seen everywhere, with high bows covered by a sagging wagonsheet. A boy drove it. A girl sat beside him. The third wagon was simply an open gray box with saddle gear piled forward in it. And at the rear, three bodies rolled softly with every bounce.

"You may as well do your doctoring here," Gonzales said. "The boys'll drive the herd up to Miles City tonight, bed down the critters in a couple of hours. They've been waiting for Miles for weeks, and I'm not going to stop them. But I had to lasso a doctor soon as possible."

Santiago followed the segundo down from the juniper-dotted bluffs toward the wagons. The chuck wagon's driver kept rolling along with the herd, but the others halted, waiting, as the restless thunder of the herd diminished ahead.

Prairie silence stretched over them as they walked their horses through the trampled bunchgrass. One of the black mules harnessed to the prairie schooner snorted and shook flies off his withers.

"Whoa!" cried the boy. A lad of twelve or thirteen, Santiago judged, burnt brown by the relentless sun. Beside him a blocky girl in a floppy felt hat, older, rose-cheeked, and immune to the sun's ravages. Her gray skirts were streaked with white dust.

"Some alkali," muttered Gonzales.

Santiago steered his bay toward the open wagon where he'd glimpsed the three helpless, supine men. He felt a rush of sadness, as he always did upon seeing mortal flesh in ruins. He had so few weapons against the destruction of flesh. Anodynes, mostly. Ways to gentle wild pain, with laudanum or paregoric or morphine. Just a few things.

"Boy! Why are we stopping? Git on with

it!" The heavy voice rose from somewhere in the covered wagon and was followed by paroxysms of coughing.

"A doctor's here, Pa."

"Well, keep going. He can git to me while we roll. We're not stopping for the devil himself."

The boy ignored him and watched as Santiago rode toward the cavvy wagon with three men lying in it.

It was not a pretty sight. The man on the left wore bloodsoaked corduroy britches, the blood brown now, and the whole area crawling with green-bellied blowflies and soft white maggots. This would be Iturbide, the gutshot one. He lay conscious, openmouthed, gummy, dehydrated, his fevered brown eyes focusing on the doctor. A rage boiled through Santiago. They hadn't even cleaned the man or given him water!

The stocky golden vaquero next to Iturbide looked equally desperate and stank of putrefaction. The left side of his young face had swollen grotesquely, puffing his lips and burying his eye in hot angry flesh. A bullet wound crawling with flies pierced his cheek, and Santiago knew the inside of the man's mouth would be ghastly. Apparently the shot had caught him openmouthed, because he could find no other hole.

16

The third man, also a Mexican, looked better. They'd slit his britches and wrapped a bandage, now black with filth, around a thigh wound. The blood had soaked it brown, and the yellow alkali dust had caked the bandage. Santiago smelled mortification under the wrapping and suspected he'd find pure hell when he pulled it off. Blood poisoning. Maybe gangrene.

"Boy! Git a-going!" cried that hoarse voice from the covered wagon. "No one stops without my say-so."

No one had stopped even to cleanse wounded men, Santiago thought grimly as he fished in his saddlebag for scissors, a knife, and his carbolic. All three of these Mexicans could well die. Why all Mexicans? Had there been a racial brawl of some sort between the Anglo hands and the Mexican ones? Did Bragg over there think so little of these Mexicans that he refused them help?

"Mr. Gonzales," he said tartly. "Get water into all of them. They've dehydrated in the heat and sun. Why weren't they put in that covered wagon?"

The answer was obvious, and Gonzales glared at him. Then he trotted off toward the river with a bucket.

"I'm Dr. Toole," Santiago said to the gutshot one. "I'll do what I can. Got to get

17

your britches down, *comprende?*"

The man nodded.

The britches refused to budge, having become a stiffened mass of blood and dust and gore. Santiago cut gingerly, amid a swarm of flies, gagging at the rank odors released when he peeled cloth away. Underneath was a sight as horrifying as any he'd seen. The man's belly swarmed with fly larvae, scores of them. A bullet had pierced the man's lower left quadrant, tearing apart intestine. Peritonitis, then: the man's whole belly cavity was swollen grotesquely and infected. He would die. With his knife blade Santiago scraped away larvae and exposed livid, discolored flesh beneath. Flies swarmed over it as fast as he scraped.

Gonzales returned and together they lifted each of the injured up and let him suck from a dipper. The three swallowed half a pail of water, slurping greedily. Even Iturbide, more than half dead, drank desperately while Santiago raged at the unseen man, Bragg, who'd been so uncaring.

"Mr. Gonzales, I have to clean his backside. Help me turn him."

Together they gently rotated old Iturbide. Maggots crawled in the exit hole just above the pelvic bone. He flooded them off with a dipperful of water and wiped the area with carbolic, feeling helpless. The wound had ceased bleeding, but an angry purple hole remained, eaten wide by larvae. He dabbed carbolic in it while Iturbide moaned and then slapped a plaster over it. He did the same with the entrance wound.

"Mr. Gonzales," he said. "Cut the man's britches away and wash him. I want every maggot off. Cut his shirt away and scrub the maggots off."

"Git a-goin' or I'll dock you half your wages," snarled that voice from the other wagon. But the boy, a brown-haired youth, had abandoned his father and stood beside the cavvy wagon, staring. Santiago spotted the heavy blonde girl coming, too.

"Miss! No. This isn't for you!"

But she ignored him, and Santiago didn't have time to argue. She stared solemnly from gray eyes that matched her dusty gray dress, saying nothing and reacting not at all to the horror and filth before her.

"What's this one's name?" he asked.

"José," responded Gonzales.

"All right, José, I have to look inside your mouth, and it's going to hurt. Can you sit up for a bit?"

José stared blankly at him. The segundo rattled something in staccato Spanish, and José, young and stocky with golden flesh bleached gray now, wrestled himself up. Santiago pried gently, unable to move the jaw more than a fraction of an inch. He could see nothing within but sensed that the whole interior of the mouth was swollen. He pried harder, turned the man's mouth toward the low sun, and dimly discerned what he needed to see. José had lost some incisors, his left molars, and two chunks of jaw. Flies crawled over the puffed-up, angry flesh and exposed white bone, swarming in and out of the hole through the cheek.

"Has he eaten anything? Had any liquids?"

"No. It's hard for him to swallow. He's been days without chow."

Santiago grunted and began cleaning the foul mess, bridling at the odors. The man ran a high fever.

"All right. Tell him I'm going to wash his mouth with something that stings. He should spit it out, not swallow it."

Santiago poured a little carbolic into the dipper and diluted it. He wished he had white vitriol. The carbolic would damage the tender flesh in the mouth and mildly poison the man if he swallowed it. Rough-and-ready medicine. Maybe bad medicine.

"Tell him again to spit it out. It's bad if he swallows it. I want him to swirl it around with his tongue if he can."

Together he and Gonzales held José up with the dipper to his lips. José did as he was asked but had trouble spitting. He leaned forward and let the frothing cleanser dribble out of his swollen lips.

Santiago sighed and plastered the hole through the cheek after wiping it down. "I want beef broth in him as soon as possible. Lots of it. Lukewarm."

"Boy! Girl! Git this wagon goin' or I'll whale your hides!" The heavy voice rolled from the wagon again and ended in another explosion of coughing.

"Young man," Santiago said, "if you want to be helpful, cut away clothing and burn it. Or start washing. I want all three of these men scrubbed clean, with soap if you have it. I don't want to see one maggot on them when you're done. Wash their hair, too, and get whatever lice you can . . ."

"I'm Apollo. This is Athena."

"Miss Athena, this isn't for you," Santiago said curtly.

"I've helped cut calves."

Santiago had no reply to that.

"Miss Athena, you heard Dr. Toole," said Jefferson Gonzales. He tried to draw her away.

She didn't budge. Santiago sliced away the britches of the third man and began unwinding the foul muslin bed sheet strangling the man's thigh.

"Who's this one?"

"Alonzo. Alonzo Montoya."

The cotton stuck to the wound. "Tell him this'll hurt," he muttered. Then he yanked swiftly. Montoya shrieked. Fresh red blood seeped through a seething mass of white worms that had eaten the bullet hole into a wide, red dish.

"Holy Mary!" cried Santiago.

The girl shrieked and began to vomit, her convulsions triggering the same reaction in them all. Santiago felt his gorge rise and knew he couldn't stop it. He found himself on hands and knees while the giant spasms of his belly pumped hot bile out of him, spraying the dun clay.

"Git a-goin'," bawled that voice. Santiago stared. From the rear of the wagon a burly, black-haired giant clambered out, his bearded face feverish and his eyes crazy. He took two steps and tumbled to the ground, roaring.

Chapter 2

The master of this cattle outfit sprawled on the clay, wheezing. Santiago Toole glanced at him sharply and decided to finish what he'd started.

"Mr. Gonzales, perhaps you could help that gentleman back into his wagon? I'll attend him directly. Miss Athena, you could help by applying cold compresses to your father if he's feverish."

The girl — well into her teens, he thought — lifted herself from the yellow earth and the pool of her bile and stared at him defiantly.

"You can't tell me what to do."

But the old segundo and the boy had reached Bragg, who lay coughing hoarsely. Santiago knew the sound and didn't like it.

He rummaged in his saddlebag for a vial of permanganate of potash then dropped a few purple crystals into a dipper of water and waited for them to dissolve. This would be a gentler antiseptic, one he could work into the small entry hole and larger exit hole without destroying tissue. He studied the wound again, dismayed. Streaks of red radiated from it like sun rays. Blood poisoning.

Something that might have been prevented if these Texas people had taken some care with the wounds. He sighed unhappily. Lister's monumental theory of sepsis and anti-sepsis had been published in 1867, in *Lancet*, but fifteen years later a knowledge of bacteria had barely penetrated the medical profession, much less laypeople.

He laved the man's thigh with the purple fluid and then gently worked it into the bullet holes, while his patient sweated and stared. If it went to gangrene, the man probably wouldn't make it. He shooed greenbottle flies off and then bandaged the thigh with cotton wraps he'd boiled sterile and kept sealed in his bag. Then he soaked the bandage with more permanganate, dyeing it purple.

At last he turned his attention to Hermes Bragg, reviewing what he knew about the last stages of consumption as he walked through lowering olive light to the covered wagon. The man's hollow, husky voice had already told him something. His larynx had ulcerated, as often happened.

In the brown shadow of the wagonsheet, the black-bearded giant glared up at him from a pallet made of grass-filled tick. Beside him the boy hunkered quietly. Jefferson Gonzales literally pinned the man down with hands on his shoulders.

"I am Dr. Toole, Mr. Bragg."

"You some deputy nosing around? Git!"

"I am sheriff of Custer County."

Consumption was a highly infectious disease, and Gonzales and the boy were both endangering themselves. "You can let him go now, sir. But before you put your hands to your face or mouth, wash them thoroughly down at the river. And you, too, son. I'll treat your father alone, now."

Santiago stared at the man before him, reading a lot. Bragg's chest had sunk just below the collarbone, and hollows had formed above it as well. Around his mouth a thick, yellow sputum had collected. Toole grasped the man's wrist and found a rapid, weak pulse. He was in the grip of hectic fever. Auscultation and percussion told Santiago all he needed to know about Bragg's gurgling lungs.

"You're slowing down the drive, Toole," the man rasped hollowly. Bragg's gaze bored up at Santiago so relentlessly it felt like a whiplash. The sheer ferocity of it rattled Toole, drove his own gaze elsewhere.

"I don't think so, Mr. Bragg. You're not in condition to go on. Have you been coughing up blood?"

Bragg nodded.

"Night sweats? Trouble breathing? Trouble

getting food past the hurt in your throat?"

Santiago knew what all the answers would be. This man's consumption had gone far beyond the lungs.

"Doctor down there told me to git to dry, cold air and git lots of exercise, keep strong. So I come."

Santiago sighed. He felt certain that exercise and a rigorous life would only hasten the course of the disease, while total bed rest might help. As for climate, he wasn't certain. There were sanatoriums in the cold, fresh air of the Swiss Alps. Some lungers seemed to improve out in the dry deserts of the southwest. But this man was dying.

"Well, no matter what your physician down there said, I'm prescribing bed rest. In Miles City. Unless you come into town and start a strict regimen of total rest and sleep, you'll be dead in a few days."

"We're a-goin' on."

"Would you mind telling me why?"

"Because I'm dying, that's why."

"You've lost me, Mr. Bragg."

Hermes Bragg coughed harshly, blood-specked sputum collecting on his lips again. The man's weakened lungs were hemorrhaging. "They know me between Big Wells and Uvalde. Ran my herds a hundred miles through there. When I put the woman out

26

she left me the care of the boy and the miss. I named them after the Greeks, like my own name." He coughed again. "I had an empire there — an empire. Walled away everything except consumption. I couldn't wall that. They told me — two doctors did — to git on north out of the steam and miasmas down there and let the cold heal up the bellows."

Toole held his tongue.

"I culled the worst and kept the best and drove on up. I'm heading for the Judith country, and I've got to get there and pick the place. When it comes to picking land most people haven't got the brains in a gnat's hind end. I'm the only one's got it. Git me there, and I'll either croak or git well, but I'll git it started to leave a legacy, leave an empire to Apollo and Athena. They'll do, along with Gonzales, but I got to git it up and going before I cash in."

"Mr. Bragg, your sole chance for that is bed rest in Miles City. You'll have to leave the empire-building to your children. From the looks of them, they're tough as rawhide."

Bragg grinned and began coughing appallingly. "They're that. I growed the girl as a boy, almost. Anything gets between her and her wishes, she goes rattler." He wheezed cheerfully.

"So I've learned."

"So we'll keep on a-goin'."

Santiago sighed. "I don't think so, Bragg. I have just treated three men with bullet holes in them. I'm holding this outfit until I get to the bottom of it."

"Oh, hell's bells, that was nothing. Some renegade Sioux, as we make it out. Eight days ago, maybe a hundred miles south. Just wanted some beeves."

"That's probably my jurisdiction, Bragg. Custer County goes on down that far from here. I'm holding your outfit here until I get the story. I'll check with the army at Fort Keogh. Find out how many Sioux got hurt. Get statements from all your men. Find out, Bragg, why all your injured are Mexican. Will you answer that?"

"Got six Mex and they was on the wrong side of the herd when the fire broke out. Dammit, Toole, you got no right to stop — "

"Consider yourself stopped. A few days will make the difference for those injured and might help you plenty."

"Forget the army. All they'll do is meddle and hold me up."

"If you ran into renegades, the army needs to know. For public safety."

"Do me a favor and let it go."

28

"Sorry, Bragg."

Bragg yelled, sitting up feverishly. "Goddam you, Toole, I'll kill you. We're gitting."

Santiago, taken aback, almost missed seeing Bragg's hand snake toward his old army Colt with astonishing speed for a man so sick. He shoved Bragg back onto his pallet.

"We'll see. We'll see," yelled Bragg.

The man slipped into some sort of convulsion, paroxysms of coughing shuddering his emaciated body. Gonzales swung into the wagonbox, glared sharply at Toole, and settled the consumptive man.

"Mr. Gonzales, this man and this outfit stay here at Miles until further notice," Toole snapped. "I'm making you responsible."

"I work for Hermes Bragg. Almost all my life. What he says I do, Toole."

Santiago had answers to that, but he set them aside. Medicine, not lawing, was needed now. Odd how the need for the one or the other rose like summer heat lightning.

"Hold him while I get some powders," he said, backing out. There seemed a fair chance Bragg would die before he dug the things he wanted from his saddlebag.

He found the belladonna, which he carried in its most powerful liquid form, the fluid extract. Because of Bragg's weakened condition he limited the dose to a drop in water and let Bragg sip. Slowly the man quieted. Santiago waited observantly, scarcely noticing the boy and girl staring at him.

September dusk lay lavender over the open prairie, and night breezes rose, flapping the wagonsheet. Santiago slid out of the Bragg wagon, while Bragg slept, his shredded lungs sucking air noisily.

"We'll drive up to Miles now," he said. "It's getting dark, but I'll lead the way. Your herd's up there somewhere, but I want to bring these injured men in. We haven't a hospital, but I have an empty jail. The town fathers don't like it when I put hospital cases in there, but I do it anyway."

"We're not sleeping in some jail!" snapped the girl.

"There's hotels, Miss. I can treat your father there."

"We'll stay in camp, like always!"

"Your father needs total bed rest indoors, out of wind and sun and heat and rain and cold."

"We'll talk it over as we go, Toole," said Jefferson Gonzales. "That wrangler driving the cavvy wagon took off, so I've got to drive it, I guess. We can certainly put those three in jail beds, if not the Braggs." He squinted at Santiago. "Unless this is some trick and you're fixing to lock up — "

30

"No, nothing like that. What do you take me for?" Toole snapped. "Unless you pull out of town I have no cause to hold you. I've got gunshot wounds here, and I'll be getting to the bottom of it. I may be presenting material to a grand jury, and there may be charges brought against some Sioux if things happened as you say. Stay around Miles — I'll help you get to good grass — and I'll do what the law has to do. It won't hurt your injured any, I might add."

"What if we don't?"

"Then you'll be fugitives from justice, and I'll come after you. A lot faster than you can move two thousand cattle."

"You can't tell us what to do."

"I'm telling you."

"I knew I didn't want no part of a doctor who packs a star," muttered Gonzales. "All right then, lead the way. All I know is the evening star and the dipper."

An hour later they reached the herd, a restless black sprawl in the night cropping grass on the benches east of the Tongue River. A half hour more brought them to camp, which was a couple of miles south of Miles City, where the trail crew waited restlessly around an amber fire that guttered in the night breezes.

The men looked surly and no wonder: a ten-minute lope would land them in cowboy paradise: saloons, hurdy-gurdies, lamplights, ladies, mattresses, tables and chairs, eggs, fresh vegetables, spices, soap, hot baths, shaves, new britches and shirts, red-eye, rattle-snake juice, popskull, and anything else that caught their fancy. Santiago smiled as he surveyed their dour faces. So far, at least, they hadn't broken discipline. They'd bedded the herd, set up camp, eaten yet another pile of sow-belly and beans, and waited.

Gonzales pulled up the cavvy wagon next to the chuck and peered about fiercely. "Snakehead, you ditched the cavvy wagon and went ahead. So I had to drive it in. You're not going to Miles tonight — you're doing night herd. Rest of you'll have to wait a little. I'm taking Mr. Bragg in and these here. Then I got a letter of credit to work out with some saloon keeper in town, and you'll each get ten dollars."

"We're owed three months!" yelled someone.

"Mr. Bragg figured if he paid you rannies now, he'd never get his herd to Judith country."

Santiago expected laughter, but no one laughed. Once again he had a sense that this outfit wasn't quite right. He peered at them in the dancing brass firelight and found them surveying him, eyes glancing from his face to his star.

"I'm Dr. Toole," he said. "I'm also sheriff here. I'm taking Mr. Bragg in for bed rest. I'm bringing in the three wounded men for medical attention. They all have grave injuries and need immediate care. Now there's something else . . ."

They waited distrustfully.

"I'll want statements from each of you. I want to know what happened, how it started, who got hurt, how many others were hurt or killed. I'll be finding out what I can from Colonel Wade at Fort Keogh directly. I'm holding all of you here, and the herd, until I know what happened and whether any laws were broken."

"You think you can hold us up, you just try it, Sheriff."

The speaker was a wiry, hollow-chested Anglo, burnt the color of walnut, and all of twenty or maybe nineteen. His hand hovered over his worn holster and a battered six-gun that dog-eared out from his thigh. His eyes glowed orange.

Santiago felt tired. "I'll deal with you later, young man. Right now I have medical matters."

"You some kind of coward, mick?"

"I know a little better than you what a hundred grains of lead will do to you, young man. You can call that cowardice if you want. I don't have the patience to worry about labels."

"Well then, we'll just forgit about taking statements, and we'll forgit about being held here, coward."

Santiago's sudden draw startled the man. One moment the sheriff was talking wearily; the next moment his Remington poked directly at the cowboy. The young man started to grab for his weapon then stopped, wild hatred flaring in his face.

Santiago slid his Remington back into his holster. He hated this part of lawing.

"You're staying, and you'll provide sworn statements, and you'll make them as truthful and complete as you can on penalty of perjury. I'll take them tomorrow." Let them raise the roof tonight, he thought. Two thousand cattle pinned them down.

He stared quietly at them all, grateful for the deftness that made him a fine surgeon — and master of the side arm.

"You'll be the other night herder tonight, Corkscrew," said Jefferson Gonzales.

The slender youth cursed bitterly. "You're dead," he said at last, his gaze daggering at Santiago Toole.

34

"From the front or from the rear?" Toole asked. It was always good to know.

"I'll face you square."

"I'll remember," said Santiago unhappily. "Mr. Gonzales, we'd better be off."

"We'll bring pa along," said Apollo Bragg. "But me and Athena are staying out here and watching the herd."

Santiago liked that boy. He was a twelve-year-old adult.

They drove quietly through the indigo dome of night while northern lights danced green on the horizon.

"What's that?" asked Gonzales.

"Northern lights."

"I never heard of that. Nothing like that in Texas."

"No, there wouldn't be."

"Some kind of storm?"

"No, it's high in the atmosphere. No one knows what makes them."

"I'll tell you what they are. They're a sign of trouble." Gonzales blessed himself. "That's a sign of wrath upon Bragg and me and this outfit."

"Why do you say that?"

But Jefferson Gonzales clammed up instantly.

"Well, tell me this. Is that youngster who made the threats going to take them seriously?"

"There's no saying. Your back's safe, at least. It'd shame him not to face you square."

Santiago grunted. Of all the silly notions that got into the heads of young hellions in the West, the notion of six-gun duels seemed the most asinine. Maybe he'd have to lock the kid up and keep him cooled down until the outfit was freed to finish its drive. That'd take some thinking out.

They struck Main Street and rode down the young evening toward the new stone jail, past somnolent saloons yellow in the cool night. The Keg. The Cottage. Brown's. At the jail Santiago lit a lamp, and then they carried old Iturbide in and eased him into a hard bunk, nothing but wooden planks and a blanket. The other two injured men hobbled in without help, stared bleakly at the iron bars in the gloomy lamplight, and then stumbled distrustfully toward other empty bunks.

Gonzales glared at Toole. "If those doors slam shut, if you've pulled some sneak — "

Santiago sighed. No one trusted doctors or sheriffs very much. He peered at the remaining cells, all empty. "Here," he said, pointing to a key on a peg behind him. "There's the key. It'll say there unless I have to lock someone up. I'm trusting you, Gonzales. You trust me."

36

The segundo plucked up the long brass key, tried a cell door with it, and slid it back on its peg. "Let's get Mr. Bragg settled," he said, sounding ashamed. "Then I'll cash the letter of credit and turn the wildmen loose. Hope you don't throw them all in the pokey before the night's gone."

But old gray Rutherford, the clerk at the Commercial Hotel, didn't want any part of it.

"This ain't a hospital, Toole," he snapped. "Get lungers in here and I lose business, and maybe folks take sick. If this one dies right here in my rooms, I'll have hell to pay with — "

"Mr. Rutherford. Have you ever heard of something called the Golden Rule?"

"What about it?" Rutherford glared, rheumy-eyed, from over his half-glasses at Toole.

"Just wondered if you'd heard of it."

Santiago turned to leave.

"Wait. You take him on over to Sylvane Tobias. If he's dying, lay him in a casket. Sylvane's got all sizes and one for this Bragg, I reckon. This here consumptive Texan can just snooze away his time in comfort. Tobias'll know when to nail down the lid. Cheaper'n a hotel, too. Now don't say I never done Bragg a favor. That's how I'd want to be treated."

Santiago smiled. "Thanks, Rutherford. I'll remember your charity."

He plunged back into the sage-scented night along with Gonzales. "I've encouraged the elders of Miles City to build me a small hospital, but they say they don't take hostages."

Gonzales laughed.

"Follow me, Mr. Gonzales. Have young Bragg follow me. We've a summer kitchen at the rear of my house. It'll be suitable this time of year, for a month anyway. I've a cot we can rig up."

A few minutes later they carried Hermes Bragg in a makeshift litter to a makeshift sickroom, while Mimi hovered at the door with a kerosene lamp.

They settled Hermes Bragg and pulled a blanket over him, while his children stared uneasily.

"Toole," the sick man rasped. "I wish Corkscrew'd shot ye dead."

Chapter 3

Santiago did his morning rounds under a white sky that rolled to the horizons like a sullen sea. The nip of fall lay in the air, and he noticed skim ice on a puddle. Miles City drowsed, a huddle of buildings lost in a western wilderness. At times like this Santiago wondered what he was doing here and had no answer. He'd drifted here like tumble-weed and stayed because nothing here reminded him of Ireland. This place lay tan and lonely and open and endless, while the great stone house to which he could never return lay in a misty valley so green it made the soul cry out in joy. This was the opposite of Kilkenny. But the hurt had dimmed now, and opposites didn't hold him here.

He wore his black frock coat today, black vest, and black holster, looking more like a mortician than a man of medicine and law. Always his morning round took him to the west end: saloon row along Park Street, closest to Fort Keogh and the soldier trade. The way saloon row looked on a quiet morning never failed to surprise him. By night it sprang alive, yellow lamplight spilling from every window onto the dirt street, seething with an animation that vanished by day. In the evenings he heard male laughter, the tinkle of upright pianos and melodeons, the swing and thump of batwing doors, and glass — always glass. Clinking, breaking, shattering. The saloons took an amazing toll of glass. Most of what went on in them was innocent, simple camaraderie, tall tales, joking, gaming. But darker entertainments might be found in some places, and these Santiago watched carefully. He knew them by their silence. The determined drunks, the obsessed gamblers, the female hustlers all seemed to congregate in silent whispery saloons where they could pursue their vices unfettered by humor or raucous cowboy fun.

This morning Park Street looked particularly forlorn. By daylight the places seemed grimy and worn and sinister. He peered into a dark hurdy-gurdy, recoiling from the smell of stale beer. No doubt Bragg's drovers had spent coin here, dancing with the ladies, drinking with girls who pushed drinks hard and sipped tea that looked like whiskey.

Santiago felt no rush to ride out to their camp and start taking statements about the Sioux fight. They'd be hung over and sullen if he went too early. So he ambled through the early white light, rattling doors, peering into dark caverns that appealed only in night-time, looking up each alley and behind buildings for drunks — and bodies. He'd found several over the years; kept some from freezing to death. Nothing this chill morning. No drunks, no murders, no knifings, no bullet wounds, no eye-gouging fights, no dead girls. It seemed almost eerie. Most trail crews hitting Miles littered the town with booze and blood and glass for days, kept the jail full of drunken brawlers; but this outfit seemed almost rigid about having its fun.

He turned back to his frame cottage on Pleasant with the medical offices in front. He had a sheriff's office now in the new jail and would stop there en route to check on his three gunshot patients. He didn't like the jail building much. It had been built of sandstone, had high, small barred windows, and could be numbingly cold even when its potbellied stove roared. He found his three patients awake and huddled in their blankets against the hard chill.

Old Iturbide looked bad. Rapid pulse. Fever. A grayness under his walnut flesh. Santiago studied the man helplessly. His kit bag of medicine had no remedies for a bullet hole through the lower abdomen. No way to fight peritonitis or put the man's intestines back together.

"How are you doing, Iturbide?"

The old man stared at him blankly.

"*No comprende,* eh?"

The old man nodded.

"I don't know Spanish, but I got a dose of Latin studying medicine. Maybe I'll try some of it. Aqua?"

"Agua, sí."

Santiago found the pail and dipper and ladled some into a tin cup. Iturbide drank thirstily.

This one hadn't eaten anything for days and probably couldn't digest much. But a good beef broth might help. Santiago sighed. He hated to burden Mimi with this.

He smiled and patted Iturbide on the shoulder, knowing the smile was a type of lie. But the weathered old man slipped his rough, hard hands around Santiago's and held the doctor desperately. The fear in those rheumy brown eyes spoke loudly to Santiago.

"*Vaya con Dios,*" Santiago said.

"*Con Dios,*" Isodoro Iturbide muttered, leaking tears down crevassed cheeks.

The weakened old vaquero let go and settled back on his hard pallet. Santiago vowed to find pillows and perhaps a tick he could stuff with straw. He wanted to make Iturbide as comfortable as possible. Since no priest resided in Miles City, Santiago was saddened that he could minister to neither body nor soul.

The others lay in the next cell, watching through the bars. He couldn't remember their names, which embarrassed him. A doctor needed to know names. He plucked up his Gladstone bag and headed for that sick bay, carefully leaving the barred cell door wide open. They watched him enter but said nothing. He rinsed out the shattered mouth of the one with white vitriol while the man groaned. Pain. From a square blue-glass bottle he poured ten drops of laudanum and slid it into the man's mouth, watching closely. In a few moments the man's face softened and then relaxed; the hurt left his brown eyes. He needed to talk with these men and that meant finding Gonzales and bringing him here.

He examined the other patient. Fever, red streaks spreading up and down the man's thigh. There was something new. He pressed his stethoscope to the man's chest, not liking the rattle he heard in the left lung. Pneumonia. He found another tattered blanket and covered the man. All he could offer the man was sleep, and that out of a bottle. Too late to amputate. He measured another small dose of laudanum and slid it down the man's throat.

"Comida," the man whispered, patting his stomach.

"All right. I'll get something."

He stepped outside, preferring the cool outdoors to the dank chill of the jail. Food. Not from Mimi, bless her. The Chinaman. Chang Loon. He trotted across Main Street and then down Tenth and up an alley to the small, red-enameled building in the rear, a grocery actually for Miles City's score or so of Celestials. He swiftly arranged for meals, half a bit each, with hot tea, broth, and rice. Chang Loon smiled, nodded, bowed, chattered in his scolding-squirrel tongue, and set to work. Santiago couldn't speak Cantonese either, but Chang Loon always managed to understand. Santiago found some two-bit pieces in his black britches and laid them on the counter. He'd bill Bragg for the chow. This wasn't a charity case.

In his own cottage he found Mimi up and spooning beef broth into Hermes Bragg, who had acute difficulty sliding the warm liquid past his ulcerated larynx. Santiago watched quietly from the doorway, loving the long, lean curve of Mimi's back and the tumult of unruly jet hair that hung loose over the shoulders of her canary-colored dress. She was French and Assiniboin, and he always thought the whole was better than the parts.

"It'll make you strong, Mr. Bragg," she said, but his response was a racking cough as his suffering lungs, filled with tubercules and hemorrhaging steadily now, spasmed again. The spray of the man's thick yellow sputum splattered Mimi, filling Santiago with sickening dread.

"Mimi! I'll take over now! Wash carefully."

The harsh tone of his voice caught her attention, and she turned to him, questions in her large eyes. She nodded, rose, and left.

"You've no right to keep me a prisoner, Sheriff!" Bragg said harshly, his voice sepulchral in a mined throat.

Santiago smiled. "You're a medical prisoner, not a sheriff's prisoner. Sentenced to bed rest."

"Where's my herd?"

"About two miles south. The grass is adequate for a day or two."

"Did my drovers have their night in town?"

"I presume so. They left no bodies around, and I arrested no drunks. Did you hire puritans, Mr. Bragg?"

Santiago eased down to the edge of the cot and checked Bragg's heartbeat with his stethoscope. Still weak and rapid. He listened once again to the man's laboring lungs and damaged heart and frowned. Bragg's caved-in

45

chest, shrunk down around his ribs, told Santiago everything. Add the man's unabated fever, the wildness in his eyes . . .

"I want you to sleep today. Nothing but sleep," he said. "But if you can manage it, I'd like you to tell me briefly what happened. The fight with the Sioux."

"I already told you."

Once again Santiago felt Bragg was holding back secrets. He'd dealt with this before, as both a sheriff and a doctor.

"How many days ago, Mr. Bragg?"

"Nine now."

"Where?"

"I can't say for certain. We were driving up the Little Powder River." He coughed again and ended up panting.

"How many?"

"A bunch. We made them out as Sioux."

"Did they want to parley? Were they asking for a beeve?"

"I don't remember. Those thieving redskins just beg a man into poverty."

"What started it?"

Hermes Bragg glared and said nothing, and Toole knew he'd run into a wall. Well, he'd get the rest from Bragg's drovers. The whole affair puzzled him more than ever.

"All right. I'll get back to this later. I want you to gargle now with white vitriol.

46

It's good for throat ulcerations and stops the putrefying. And then I'll give you a small amount of belladonna, which is an anti-spasmodic that'll help. You're too weak for anodynes. I'll be seeing some patients and then riding out to your cattle camp. I want the story from you when I return. I'll have it from your drovers, but I want it from you."

"They won't — " Bragg stopped himself. "Let us go, Toole, or I'll have them tree this town. Maybe you'll be doctoring yourself — if you live."

"You're a friendly gent, Bragg. It starts a sheriff to wondering."

Santiago finished his dosing and left with another volley of coughing behind him. He feared for his own health and Mimi's and hastened away. In the kitchen he poured some warm water from the stove reservoir into a basin and washed carefully, dreading the contagious bacilli that managed to live long periods outside of the human body.

Mimi watched thoughtfully. "You're being very careful, Santo."

"Yes, and you must be, too, Mimi. People with Indian blood have even less resistance to it."

"Ah, Santo! The French are immune to everything except love!"

He laughed.

"You have two people waiting," she said. "Mrs. Crowfoot and one from the railroad I don't know."

He treated Mrs. Crowfoot's thin blood with a prescription of three grains of citrate of iron daily and the suggestion she eat a lot of red meat. The railroad man turned out to be Homer Neven, the telegrapher and stationmaster at the new Northern Pacific depot. Neven, a stocky man going to fat, suffered a severe bowel obstruction that epsom salts hadn't relieved. Santiago debated using something drastic, such as gamboge, but decided against it because it evoked nausea and vomiting. He decided instead on Culver's root and prescribed fifteen drops of the fluid extract. If Neven didn't find relief, he was to return in the morning.

"Oh, Neven. I have a telegram to send. Sheriff business," Santiago said. "Mind if I scribble it out now?"

"Good a time as any. Nothing but a through freight until three."

Santiago had grown impatient with nib pens, so he penciled the words on a piece of foolscap and handed it to Neven. "This goes on down to the sheriff at Uvalde, Texas. I hope I spelled that right. I want all the information I can get on Hermes Bragg. Be sure to sign me Sheriff of Custer County,

48

Montana Territory."

Neven read it and nodded. "That's the outfit here now?"

"It is."

"Looks like an outlaw bunch to me. Those cowboys came in last night quiet as mice, they tell me. Now, you ever heard of cowboys hitting the saloons like deacons at a prayer meet? I never did. So they're all crooked as all get-out. That's what folks are saying. Afraid to lift a mug of beer if it loosens up a tongue or two. I hear you got three locked up."

"No, Neven, no one's locked up. That's three injured in there because Miles City's got no hospital."

"Gunshot, I hear. Three punctured greasers. Being fed by the Chinaman."

"Where'd you hear that, Neven?"

"Why, Rutherford told Sylvane Tobias that this Bragg's about to expire, and Tobias went hunting you at the jail house and found three shot greasers and told everyone. Tobias said you got careless and left the cell doors open, so he slammed them shut and locked 'em, which is the only thing to do with greasers."

"They aren't prisoners, and they deserve your respect!"

"Well, whatever they be, Tobias got them

49

penned up proper. I hate to think of dagos on the loose."

Fuming, Santiago dismissed Neven and stalked over to the jail, where he found the three Mexicans glowering behind locked cell doors. He freed them and pocketed the key this time, trying to figure out enough Spanish words to explain. Old Iturbide looked too sick to care, but the others glared at him in the gloom.

It was getting along toward noon. Time to ride out to the cow camp and take statements. If things checked out, maybe he'd just release them to continue on up to the Judith country. He couldn't hold a herd long unless he had powerful reasons. Every day he delayed them Bragg lost wages for eighteen or twenty men. He'd keep Bragg here, though, one way or another.

In his small barn behind the house he led his bay Irish thoroughbred, St. James, into the aisle and brushed the summer-sleek animal until he shone. Then he threw a blanket and big western saddle, one made right there in Miles City, over the sixteen-hand animal and cinched him up tight. He slipped a snaffle bit into the bay's mouth and buckled the throatlatch of the bridle. Then he checked his two saddlebags.

In the house he found his wide-brimmed

black hat and paper and pencil and paused to kiss Mimi. He loved to sneak up on her and buss her happily. She always turned passionate, even when she was beating carpets.

"Oh, Santo," she breathed. "What's the hurry?"

"I've got to take statements. Maybe stop at Keogh to talk to Wade afterward. Look, Mimi — don't get too close to Bragg. He sprays consumption like a fountain, eh?"

"Maybe I'll come with you, Santo. I've never seen a cow camp."

He stared at her and laughed. She primly untied a bib apron and dried her hands, grinning at him.

Santiago knew better than to argue. What Mimi set her heart on, Mimi got. Instead he unsaddled St. James and harnessed old Mick, the gray trotter, to the buggy. She appeared miraculously, white parasol in hand, as he buckled the last of the breeching and backed Mick into the shafts. He tossed his saddlebags into the buggy and steered Mick out under an overcast sky toward the Tongue River.

"Tell me about them, Santo."

"Not much to tell," he said, enjoying the quiet progress up the river and the feel of the light buggy under the quilted leather seat. "A couple thousand longhorns coming up to Montana grass. This one started down in south Texas, some place called Uvalde. Bragg's doctor told him to head for a cold, dry climate so he came. He said he hopes this country will cure him, but if it doesn't, he wants to get a place started for his children. He's got two children with him, boy and girl. The girl's well into her teens. They got into a scrape with some Sioux down on the edge of the county, maybe in Wyoming, and they're all tight-mouthed about it. Afraid I'll cause them trouble, I guess. So I'll get some statements — I have to account for three bullet holes — and then I'll let them go. It costs Bragg plenty for me to hold his men and herd, and I have no real reason to except to get some information."

"Mr. Bragg was so feverish, I thought maybe he was mad."

"That's hectic fever, Mimi. He knows he's dying, and he's rigid about everything. Powerful, dominant men get like that at the last."

"Would he have lasted longer in Texas, Santo?"

"Probably. If he'd taken to bed. Given his temperament, he probably would have killed himself as fast down there as up here. I'd say this whole journey didn't help him at all."

"Look, Santo! It looks like a buffalo herd!"

They rounded a shoulder of dun prairie and found themselves staring at a vast herd of cattle. But unlike the black buffalo, these animals had been tinted by a mad painter: brown, dun, red, black, white, yellow, and orange. They grazed quietly, fattening on tan shortgrass, cured by Montana's dry August and September. Santiago noted a large HB road brand on the left shoulders and other, less decipherable brands on their flanks.

Ahead, on the bottoms next to the river, stood the Bragg camp. Santiago steered Mick toward the camp, feeling a great silence there. The breeze said nothing. Neither did the cropping longhorns. The low river rippled gloomily, silver in the overcast. Lounging men watched Santiago and Mimi pull in just as silently, until Jefferson Gonzales arose, brushed grit off his worn chaps, and welcomed them.

"How's Mr. Bragg, Sheriff?" he asked first off.

"Unchanged but resting quietly. The others are much the same, but resting and getting the help they need."

"This your lady?"

"This is Mimi, my wife. She's never seen a trail herd or a cow camp."

"Well, now you have," said Gonzales shortly.

"We may as well get right on with it, Mr. Gonzales. Why don't you just send the men over one at a time, and I'll write what they have to say. They can either sign or put an *X* at the bottom."

Gonzales looked discomfited. "We've been talking among ourselves, Sheriff. What we went and done is draft a statement ourselves, Miss Athena wrote it out, and we all signed or made our mark, me notarizing the marks. Here."

Gonzales thrust a battered sheet at Santiago. On it was a brief pencilled statement in a stern, sharp hand and a long list of names. He read.

September 5, 1882. Nine days ago we were attacked by a band of renegade Sioux, number uncertain, on the Little Powder River. We defended at once to preserve the herd, but we were outnumbered. We hit several and they got three of us. They got no beef and we continued on our way. Signed . . .

Santiago scanned the list, looking for any name he knew, any name on a dodger, and found none. He read it again, annoyed, learning nothing he didn't already know.

"Will that do it for you, Sheriff?"

Santiago sighed. "Afraid not, Mr. Gonzales. I'll want to talk to each man separately."

Then came a new voice, higher and feminine. "It's all you're going to get, Sheriff." Santiago looked up and found himself staring at Miss Athena. "Take it or leave it. I've ordered my men to break camp and leave."

She glared at him defiantly, daring him to say no. He realized he confronted a big girl, a bundle of pure will, square-faced and square-bodied with gray eyes and ruddy cheeks. If young Apollo seemed a man, this girl seemed even more of one.

"I'm afraid not, Miss Bragg. Maybe in an hour or two, if I get detailed accounts of what happened."

"Like hell," she snapped. "Just try it."

Circled around him, standing jauntily but wire-sprung and ready, stood a dozen of Bragg's men, all armed, all watching him lazily from unfriendly faces.

Chapter 4

Santiago found himself confronting a dozen armed men. He knew Mimi sat in the black buggy watching, her hands in her reticule, no doubt clutching her little revolver. She'd backed him two or three times but not against a mob of Texas drovers with their bark on.

"Miss Bragg," he said, "you're young — fourteen is it? — and perhaps you don't understand that impeding an investigation by an officer of the law is — "

"Arrest me," she retorted.

Holy Mary, he thought. A spitfire. He turned to the segundo. "Mr. Gonzales, perhaps you'll assist me?"

"We ride for the brand, mister. If you don't know Texans, you can corral that about us right now. We stick with the brand."

Santiago was puzzled. Why the confrontation? He wanted details about a scrape with some renegade Indians and ran into this. He peered at one man and then the next, memorizing each of them. They were the breed, all right, rough as cobs, weathered chestnut, leaned down to rawhide by hard living and poor chow, ragged, worn, with cold-steel hell in their eyes. Whether they'd actually murder a sheriff he didn't know.

"Would you mind explaining why you won't tell about a scrape with some Indians?"

"We'd mind."

"You make me wonder if you're concealing something."

No one blinked.

He addressed Athena. "Miss Bragg. You are going nowhere with this herd. Until I have statements, you'll stay put. You can't run a herd fast enough to outrun a posse, and if you run, I'll run faster. Run, young lady, and the law runs before you and behind you and at the side of you. I'm as fast as a telegraph. You and your hands will find the Custer County jail will hold you all."

She grinned defiantly. "We'll see."

"Now, you haven't asked me about your father, lass. Or the three others."

"He's dying. Send us the news up the trail when it happens."

The girl's nonchalance stunned him. She stared, hard-eyed, but the boy, Apollo, faltered for the briefest moment.

"Let's talk about love, Miss Bragg. A daughter's for her father. Her father's for the apple of his eye."

"Let's not."

"Do you think you're doing your father's will?"

"I'm a Bragg, and I'm looking after Bragg property."

"He needs you at his side."

"If I didn't keep on going, he'd shoot me dead, and that's the truth."

"Is that how he raised you, Miss Bragg?"

"Property's hard to hang on to."

"You said he'd shoot you?"

"He's hard and I'm hard and Apollo's hard. Soft people are always losers."

"I'm a soft person, Miss Bragg. I try to heal the sick and help those in need and bring justice to criminals and help their victims."

"And you're a loser."

"I think you'd better come visit your father this afternoon. He needs you now."

"No, he doesn't. He always said, when a horse breaks a leg, put it out of its misery and keep on going. *Keep on going.*"

This girl shocked him.

"Very well. I'm on my way to Fort Keogh, Miss Bragg. Renegade Sioux are army business. Colonel Wade will no doubt send soldiers out to talk with you. Would you or your brother like to come with me?"

She glared stonily.

He clambered into his buggy and lifted the reins.

"Stop him!" she cried.

But none of them was quite that loyal to the brand. Santiago studied them all, looking for the one who'd backshoot a sheriff. Then he flipped the reins, and Mick broke into a smart trot. He distanced himself from the Bragg camp swiftly, and only when he reached the edge of the herd did he realize he hadn't seen the one called Corkscrew.

"I hate to see you backed down," muttered Mimi angrily.

He grinned. "So do I."

"They think you're weak now."

"I think they know better than that. They can count. One of me, thirteen of them plus two reckless children."

"Why are they so quiet? What are they hiding, Santo?"

"I wish I knew. I think maybe Colonel Wade has some answers. Probably they don't want to admit to killing some Indians. This scrape — it didn't happen the way they say it did. But I don't know, and I've got nothing but a few intuitions about it."

He drove north, past the herd grazing quietly in the dun bunchgrass. A couple of the animals showed bright pink flesh in the furrows of the road brand, while others had haired over. He thought of fording the lazy Tongue River, running murky and tan this dry month, but decided not to try because of quicksand. Instead he steered Mick up the old trail toward the log bridge connecting Keogh with Miles City and then rolled across it, the noise of Mick's hooves hollow on the heavy gray planks.

On a bronze bench to the west lay the fort, baking in the morning haze. Nelson Miles had planted the fort there, and another fort called Custer over on the Big Horn River, in the heart of Sioux country as a continuing presence of bluecoat power. Now Keogh was gradually transforming itself from drafty frame buildings into solid tan brick ones with mansard roofs, even as Miles City had become a solid prairie metropolis boasting white-washed frame cottages and false-front stores and a growing population catering to the army, the railroad, and the new cattle empires of the plains.

They drove parallel to the silvery rails that now pierced westward as far as a camp called Livingston. Next year those steel rails were supposed to be connected with others thrusting eastward from Oregon, and the Northern Pacific would span the continent. He hoped no train would come. Mick went crazy at the thunder of them and had almost wrecked the buggy, not to mention Dr. Toole.

He steered the rocking buggy past the outbuildings, the powder magazine, a howitzer pointed eastward along the flank of the cold clear Yellowstone, and into the parade, dry and dusty from want of rain. He liked the place no more than he did earlier. Ever since he'd warned Colonel Orville Prescott Wade about the scheming of his own sergeant major a couple of years earlier, Wade had been nasty and more condescending than ever, having no use at all for civilian lawmen.

Santiago parked the buggy at the headquarters building on officers' row before a flapping flag and the guidon of the Fifth Infantry. He dropped a carriage weight to hold Mick, though Mick didn't need restraining, and lent an arm to Mimi. He loved to bring Mimi here, show her off. She always turned Indian when she came here as a sort of defiance. As he helped her alight he swore she'd become all Assiniboin and belonged in fringed doeskin.

The current sergeant major, a thin, acerbic man, nodded and ushered them into Wade's office. The pale, balding commanding officer folded his Ned Buntline dime novel and stood.

"Why, it's Dr. Toole and his squaw. Or is it Sheriff Toole? I never know."

"Sheriff Toole this time, Colonel. Her name is Mimi. For you, it's Mrs. Toole."

"Yes, yes. A little joke. Then you're here

on business, I take it."

"Just a question, Colonel. Have you any information on a shooting scrape between some Sioux off the reservation in Dakota and some cattle drovers? The last week or ten days?"

The colonel blinked owlishly and shook his head.

"We've a herd up from Texas. You can almost see it from here, and you're no doubt aware of it. A big one. Owned by a man named Hermes Bragg from southern Texas, Uvalde. He's gravely ill and under my care. But they also brought in three drovers, all Mexican, with gunshot wounds. One looks very bad — shot through the lower abdomen — but the other two might make it. If one survives blood poisoning and escapes gangrene."

"I suppose they claim Sioux did it. The gunshot wounds."

"They're saying about that much and nothing more. I can't get a word out of them."

"Texans are like that, Sheriff."

"This supposedly happened nine days ago, down on the Little Powder, about a hundred miles south. Maybe my jurisdiction, maybe Wyoming. They're not saying anything more. One thing, though. All three of the wounded men are Mexican. It makes me wonder if they had a quarrel. And if they did, whether they buried a drover or two along their trail somewhere. They sure aren't talking, and the Braggs are keeping a lid on."

"The Braggs?"

"Daughter and son. A spitfire of a girl all those drovers obey just as if old Bragg himself gave the orders. Bragg himself's at my house, sinking by the hour from consumption."

Wade steepled and unsteepled his hands, as was his wont, and frown lines collected on his pale, blue-tinted forehead. "There's still renegades around, no doubt of it. We get reports now and then. Immigrants think it's over, and it isn't. Scalpings, mutilations, other troubles, mostly theft though. Reservation life's hard on 'em, especially with the buffalo shot away and not enough food because the confounded Indian agents and the blasted government — "

"But no reports of trouble? Nothing from Fort Robinson?" asked Santiago impatiently.

For an answer Wade summoned his adjutant, Lieutenant Mandrake Gillespie. "Have we a bronco incident? Go talk to the telegrapher, Lieutenant."

The slat-thin young man vanished down a hallway.

"Another thing, Colonel. I suggested they report this scrape to you so you could notify the Pine Ridge Sioux agency. But they wouldn't, and I had a sense that they didn't want you to know. I ran into a wall. In fact, I ran into obstruction."

Wade grinned. "What you need is a little army muscle, Sheriff. Since this is an Indian scrape, I suppose we have some jurisdiction here. If some of those young broncos busted loose to hunt down some beef and shoot up a few settlers, then we'll get cracking. We can't have that. They've got a tribal herd over at Pine Ridge now, courtesy of Uncle Sam, but it's not enough. Not enough meat, not like the old Buffalo days. Still, they're not starving, far as I know. They've no cause to go raiding trail herds except for the pure deviltry of it. They got that still, the deviltry."

"Would you be so kind as to wire Fort Robinson, sir?"

"They'd have wired us, Sheriff. They report all incidents to this command."

Santiago sighed. "Well, I'll wire them myself from town, then."

Wade laughed nastily.

The adjutant returned. "Nothing, sir. No report of any trouble."

"There. You see, Sheriff? There's been no Indian trouble."

"There's always broncos, Colonel."

Wade steepled his hands again, corrugating

64

his forehead with thought. "I suppose it's occurred to you that Indians are blamed for all sorts of things they don't do."

"It's occurred to me."

"Well, then," said Wade effusively, "you have your answer. All you have to do is make them talk."

"Bragg's at my house. And I can't get a word out of him. The three wounded Mexicans are at the jail — only hospital I've got — and I don't have a translator handy. They're all in bad shape, Colonel, and they're my patients, two of them on the brink of dying, and — "

"You're too soft, Toole. Always too soft. The doctoring always gets in the way of your sheriffing."

"Just the opposite, Colonel. I'm a lot better sheriff because I'm a doctor."

"Too soft, Toole."

It was an old taunt. Half the population of Miles City believed it. Let a doctor try to bandage or heal a criminal or crazy cowboy or wildman, and half the town said he was too soft, too easy on crime. He'd quit letting it nettle him. At first it had been aimed at his Irish upbringing. Too soft. Son of a rich Irish baron. Then at his medicine. How can some damned doctor and his Hippocratic oath shoot a bandit? But he'd always done what

65

he had to do in either office, law or medicine, and he'd grown accustomed to the barbs.

"Soft enough to pull bullets out of you, Colonel."

Wade blinked.

Santiago knew it was time to get out. "If you learn of an incident, send me the news by messenger," he said curtly. He gathered Mimi and wheeled out, past the saturnine sergeant and the alert adjutant.

He drove home silently, wondering why this army he was forced to deal with constantly loathed the slightest intervention from civilian authority.

Mimi broke the silence. "Do you think it was a scrape with the Sioux?" she asked.

"Ask me other questions."

"Why don't you just let them go?"

That was one he'd been asking himself, too. "I suppose I will," he muttered. "I can't hold that herd while I fish around for some hint of a crime."

They drove back to Miles quietly, the resolution thickening in him to let the Bragg outfit go. He had no reason to hold them. A sheriff who jailed people on suspicion was a sheriff who violated the rights of those people. He'd encountered this sort of thing before: something wrong but no real evidence of crime. Except for three men with bullet holes in them . . .

In the aisle of his small barn he unbuckled Mick's harness and then rubbed down the old gray before pitching him a forkload of prairie hay. Time to look in on Bragg and the others and then do his evening rounds. Mimi would have supper for him soon. Dear, patient Mimi. Her food sat on the Majestic stove and dried out or burned or cooled while he doctored and sheriffed. One expected a sheriff or doctor to have an irregular life, but his was doubly irregular.

He found Bragg alert in his cot in the summer kitchen, but a ghastly rattle accompanied each painful breath. Santiago found fever on the man's brow. His extremities were cold. He listened to the man's tortured breathing and the arrhythmic spasms of a weakening heart and grunted.

Bragg grinned, his emaciated face macabre, his gaze raking the doctor.

"I've decided to let the herd go, Bragg."

Bragg's response was a paroxysm of coughing.

"You're hiding something. So are your men. So are your children."

Bragg laughed, a strange, sepulchral rattle. "You're costing me money. I should bill you for the delay, Toole."

"Your daughter says she won't come in

to see you. I suppose your boy feels the same way. She says that's how you'd want it — keep on going. Horse breaks a leg, shoot it."

"That's my girl. That's how I raised her up."

"Let's talk about love, my friend."

The man coughed and wheezed, laughter convulsing him painfully.

"Love ain't nothing but soft emotion. But property's real. When they get that herd on the Judith grass, they'll be plumb respected in the territory."

"That's what she seemed to think, Bragg. Does she like you?"

"Never asked her. I'd be putting the whip to her if she did. I don't want some damn soft streak to wreck her. Live hard, be hard, and you win easy."

"You're not winning, Bragg."

"I already won, Toole. I ain't some flunky tradesman like you with hardly a penny. I got a fortune out there, beef, and two Braggs to build it bigger. They're harder than me even. Tougher'n me, Toole. They know Braggs from east to west in Texas, and you'll know Braggs here in Montana just as big."

"You ever care about anyone, Hermes Bragg?"

The man laughed, convulsing again, spraying the air with the tubercular bacilli.

"Your men are loyal to you," Toole persisted.

"I scare 'em half to death. Those that disobey get a bullet for pay."

"Is that what happened to the Mexicans?"

Bragg coughed and laughed again. "You never quit trying, do you, Toole?"

"Army says it got no report of any fight. The Sioux agent at Pine Ridge, over in the corner of Dakota, lets the army know if he hears anything, or he's got wounded Sioux, or his tribal police pick up something. So, Bragg, no fight. It was something else."

Bragg wheezed. But his gaze riveted on Santiago, lashing the doctor. Toole had never encountered a glare so mesmerizing and somehow frightening. It had physical force, the power of a battering ram in it. Never before had a man forced him to gaze elsewhere, anywhere, just so long as he didn't have to meet that unendurable force. He compelled himself to peer back at this emaciated giant but couldn't hold his gaze, and it slid away, making him feel like a scolded boy. Holy Mary, he thought. What sort of brute was this?

Santiago dropped his stethoscope into his pigskin bag. He decided against medicines now. The man had weakened in just one day. "Mr. Bragg," he said quietly, "would you like a minister? There's a Presbyterian. And a Methodist circuit rider comes through frequently."

"That's the soft stuff, Toole. I never held with it. One of those vultures comes around praying over me, I swear I'll rise up out of my box and poke my fist down his throat."

"That would be gratitude, Bragg."

"Toole. All those things: Love. Gratitude. Mercy. They're snares for fools. Don't waste any on me."

"I'm trying not to, Mr. Bragg. Who do I bill for your care and the care of your three wounded men?"

"Shoot 'em. I didn't give you the say-so to care for them. Shoot 'em, Toole. And if you stick a Bragg for boxes and burying, she'll ignore you."

The man glared at him from fevered eyes.

"One thing puzzles me, Mr. Bragg. How come they're loyal? You're disloyal to them. It's not fear that keeps them loyal. Not with you lying here. They act like they love you, Bragg. That's the word all right, love. They're proud to ride with Hermes Bragg."

"Go away, Sheriff." Bragg shuddered and slid into another paroxysm that rattled his whole body and left him panting. Tears welled in his eyes. "Git out!" he raged. "Git out!"

Chapter 5

Lamplight ambered the window of his jail office, and a wiry horse stood hipshot and weary at the hitch rail. Company, then. Santiago paused a moment to study the brand in the lavender dusk. He couldn't quite make it out. He entered his office at the front of the sandstone building and discovered Jefferson Gonzales back in the cells, along with Chang Loon.

Good enough, thought Santiago. He wanted to have a long talk with Gonzales.

"Mr. Gonzales, how are our patients?"

The segundo peered sharply at him and shook his head slowly. "You'd better start with Isodoro, Doctor."

Back in the other cell, Chang Loon was ladling a steaming broth of some sort into bowls for the other two — José somebody and Alonzo somebody, he remembered now. The Chinaman looked up, babbled something incomprehensible, and shook his head sadly.

In the cell where old Isodoro Iturbide lay, Santiago felt a change. He never knew just what he sensed in these cases, only that the Dark Angel hovered near, awaiting the last ticks of God's clock. The old man lay shriveled

— why did mortals shrink at death? — and quiet, conscious, and staring from dulled brown eyes. Breath came irregularly, in fits, with long tendrils of silence between. Santiago took his hard, dark hand and found it cold.

Jefferson Gonzales entered quietly and stood next to the cot.

"He asked for a priest, Dr. Toole. But there's none, yes?"

"There's none in Miles. One reaches the fort now and then on an army circuit. I'm always told of his presence, Mr. Gonzales."

"Then Isodoro leaves us unshrived. He has things to say. . . ."

"Does he leave anyone behind? Does he wish us to notify anyone? Has he any messages?"

Gonzales shook his head. "He mumbled something. He said he's afraid. That he will go to *infierno* — ah, hell. Then he wept."

"And did you assure him, Mr. Gonzales?"

But that strange silence Santiago had felt from the moment he'd met these Bragg people descended, and the blue-eyed segundo stared at the blank stone wall.

Santiago stood. "Sit here on the cot beside him and hold his hand, Mr. Gonzales. There's no other comfort for him but the hand of a friend."

Wordlessly Gonzales slipped down beside

the old vaquero and put his own hands over the cold one. Something tugged at Santiago, some sense that Iturbide had left messages after all, messages not for a sheriff's ears.

He picked up his black medical valise and headed over to the next cell. His other two Mexican patients ate noisily in the lamplight with Chang Loon's help. Alonzo Montoya. That was the name of the one shot through the thigh. He looked a little better tonight after another day's bed rest. The man's forehead seemed cooler, too. Santiago studied the flesh around the bandaged area, sensing some small improvement, but he couldn't be sure in the low amber light of the kerosene lamp.

"Bueno," he said. He could convey that much. *Bueno, malo.* The gaunt man smiled slightly.

The third man was sucking broth ladled by Chang Loon through the ruin of his mouth, so Santiago waited. The flesh around the cheek wound had turned purple and yellow, making the cowboy look worse than he probably was. That one had the best chance. Even now he sat up comfortably while the Chinaman fed him.

"Dr. Toole," said Jefferson Gonzales.

Santiago slipped back to Iturbide's cell and found the quietness he expected. Iturbide's eyes had closed. He placed a stethoscope to the old vaquero's chest and heard nothing.

"Gone."

"He didn't deserve it."

"Being killed, Gonzales?"

The segundo nodded and withdrew his hand from the lifeless one.

Santiago stood. "I'll leave you three with him. I've some records to fill out in my office. When you're ready, help me fill them out. Name, age, next of kin, all that. I'll also want to know what is to be done with him."

Gonzales nodded, and Santiago slipped to his sheriff's quarters on the street side of the building. He hardly knew what to do. He had a star and a medical degree, and he felt as helpless before death as a child. Still, there might be something, he thought.

"*Pater noster,*" he mumbled, "*qui es in caelis, sanctificetur nomen tuum. Adveniat regnum tuum. Fiat voluntas tua sicut in caelo et in terra. . . .*" Our Father, who art in Heaven . . .

It came to him at the end that death could be a cause for rejoicing, not grief. Still, the man had died perhaps fifteen hundred miles from his home, alone, in tears, in pain, of a bullet . . . and fearing hell. There were better deaths.

Jefferson Gonzales interrupted his somber train of thought, sitting down quietly on the other side of the battered desk.

"Are the others taking it well?"

"They're afraid. They fear the mortification of their flesh. And the ghost. Can we move Iturbide?"

"That's one of the things to discuss, Jeff. May I call you Jeff?"

"Call me Jefferson."

"I can notify Sylvane Tobias, our mortician. But I gather the Braggs won't pay. Hermes advised me to shoot those gentlemen back there."

Santiago waited quietly, wondering much. Gonzales grimaced.

"He's always talked that way, with the bark on, and did the opposite. Until recently. The sicker he got, the more serious he was about all that. Before he took sick he'd say, 'Shoot that horse,' but then he'd put a splint on it and let it heal up lame and pension it."

"Pension it?"

"Ranch talk. Put it out on pasture to live to old age after a useful life."

"I take it Hermes Bragg said one thing and did another."

"Mostly, Doctor. Mostly. Sometimes he had to show he meant it, and then he'd be hard and mean for a while. Then he got sick, and he turned hard, period."

"Well, that answers one of my questions, Jefferson."

"Are you a doctor or is this a sheriff investigation?" Gonzales retorted sharply.

"Neither. A man can't help wonder why your outfit sticks with a man that abuses them. Or a girl that's hell on everyone. Maybe you've got memories of a different Bragg."

"You got forms to fill out?"

"Jefferson, you can't keep a man from wondering, now, can you?"

"You just write and I'll get going. I've got to get night herding organized. And find grass tomorrow. And when the hell are you going to let us go?"

"I want to talk about that. Soon, I think." Santiago picked up his county-owned nib and jabbed it into an inkpot. "All right then, full name, age if you know it, kin if you know them."

Gonzales barked out replies, and Santiago scratched, cursing the inventor of steel nibs. No known kin. From west of Big Springs, Texas. Cause of death . . . gunshot wound in lower left abdomen, on or about August 24, 1882, in vicinity of Little Powder River and Wyoming line.

"Who shot him, Jefferson?"

The segundo's face turned stony. "Sioux."

76

Santiago dipped his nib and scribbled and blotted and cussed and then was done. Isodoro Iturbide became a line in a ledger book.

"Do I summon Tobias?"

"Yes. If Bragg won't, we will. We'll ante up. We didn't spend hardly nothing. No one felt like it, so we got — "

"That's what I heard, Jefferson. You'd think some cowboys months out on the trail would whoop it up a little, wouldn't you? But they tell me you all downed one or two beers, bought a few duds and things, and filed out. Left half the merchants and saloon keepers peeved."

"With three wounded, why should we celebrate?"

Santiago shrugged. "I never knew that to stop a cowboy."

"I get the feeling you're digging, Toole. I think I'm talking to a doc and it turns out to be a sheriff."

"This Bragg outfit makes a man curious, Jefferson."

The segundo sat glowering at him across the lamplight, not wanting to leave and not liking the questions. "You said you were going to let us go?"

"I think so. I've no reason to hold you, and I can't tie down a herd while I fish for one."

"When?"

77

Santiago smiled gently. "You want to leave Iturbide for me to bury, or get out?"

Somehow the question took Gonzales aback. "Miss Athena will want to go."

"And what do you and the others want?"

Jefferson grinned crookedly for a reply. "If you spring us at dawn, I'll have a fight. If you spring us at noon, and this Tobias can get a box ready and a hole dug in the morning, then it'll work out."

"I'll ride out and release you at noon. Unless something comes up to change that, Gonzales."

"You've been calling me Jefferson all evening, Sheriff."

"This star here says I'm that, and I take it as seriously as my medicine."

Gonzales nodded.

"You people are hiding something from me. I'm going to find out what. And when I do, I'll catch up with you if I have reason. It may be up on the Judith, but I'll catch up with you if there's need."

"For a doctor, you talk pretty good sheriff, Toole."

"Think it over, Gonzales. I'll release the herd, but it doesn't mean any of you are free."

Gonzales nodded somberly and stood. "Get Tobias. We'll make it up some way, the

78

outfit will. And Doc — thanks."

Santiago watched him vanish into the indigo night. Mosquitos drilled in through the door, whining toward the lamp. He liked that man.

Santiago leaned back in his swivel chair, mulling over what he'd learned, trying to make it fit. But nothing made any sense. He sighed, rose, walked back to the cell where Iturbide lay, and gazed quietly, aware that the wounded men in the next cell stared at him. Death always reminded him of his own mortality and the thousand ways a man could die. Here was a soul gone, the man and his life a mystery. Who was his mother? Had he sisters and brothers? Did anyone grieve? He could not have helped the man. But death always reminded him he belonged to a profession that won a few battles but lost every war. Maybe some day medicine would win a lot of battles. Joseph Lister alone had transformed his calling.

He left the jail, feeling the nippy night air tug at his frock coat. Sylvane would be in his apartment now, so he walked east down Main Street to the cabinetmaker's shop, down an alley to its rear where the apartment was tacked on, and knocked. Lamplight in the windows told him he'd find Tobias there.

"It's you," said Tobias.

"I've interrupted your dinner, Sylvane. This'll just take a moment. One's gone. The old Mexican, Isodoro Iturbide. The crew says they'll pay for a box and burying if you'll get it done pronto, first thing in the morning. I'd be obliged if you'd collect the deceased tonight. It's a little hard on the other two to have him there."

"Everybody's in a rush," Tobias grumbled. "Where'm I going to find a gravedigger now? I'll have to start a Mex section on the hill, too."

"Why?"

"We can't be laying Mex next to whites, Toole."

"Why?"

"Just not done is why."

"You have a Catholic plot. Put him there."

"But next to whites, Toole?"

"I don't suppose God cares, Sylvane."

"Well, everyone else does! I'll finish my chicken and go harness Hell and — "

"Harness Heaven, Sylvane." The undertaker had three harness horses, a black named Hell, a gray named Purgatory, and a dappled white named Heaven.

"I'll do what's fitting, Santiago. Plain pine box, I suppose. You going to do some papist mumbo jumbo, or do I read?"

Santiago laughed. "Set it for ten in the

morning. I'm going to let that outfit go around noon."

He left Tobias muttering on his porch and headed to the west end to ask some questions. With Iturbide dead he had a murder on his hands, and he intended to get to the bottom of it.

The night breeze whipped up dust and dried manure on Main Street and peppered Santiago's face with it. Miles and Strevell's hardware sign hanging from chains seesawed and clattered. Santiago headed into the wind, wishing he'd worn his buffalo coat even though it was early September. The farther he headed toward the west-end saloons, the worse it got, until he thought nature conspired against him. The evening was young, and it seemed a good time to talk to a few barkeeps.

The batwing doors creaked as he turned into the Cottage Saloon and headed toward the good mahogany bar with its mirrored backbar. The odor of sour beer struck him.

When asked about the cowboys, the barkeep replied that the Bragg outfit hadn't come in. They'd all marched into the Grey Mule for an hour and then marched out into the night.

So Santiago headed down Park Street and found the Grey Mule almost empty. There were only a few blue-shirted noncoms from Fort Keogh drinking in the yellow light from wagon-wheel chandeliers and arguing the merits of the trapdoor Springfield.

"What'll it be, Sheriff?"

"A draft beer, Murphy."

He watched the barman in the dirty white apron draw a beer, let the foam roll down the side of the white mug, and drop it wetly on the shiny worn bar. Santiago dug for a nickel and found a dime.

The noncoms at the table noticed Santiago's steel star and stared. The sheriff was well-known to all the sergeants at Fort Keogh.

"Got a moment, Murphy?"

"I got nothing but time tonight, Sheriff."

"Were you working last night?"

"I sure was." The man turned cautious, his watery blue eyes suddenly wary. "Some trouble? Nothing like that here, Toole."

"No, no trouble. I take it the Bragg outfit came in here."

"The cowboys, yes, and they spent less than any mother's son of a cowboy ever spent in here coming off the trail. Strangest thing a man ever did see."

"I'd like to hear about it, Murphy."

"Not worth telling, Sheriff. But trade's so dull tonight I got nothing better to do than bore the socks off you. Yeah, they came in

after their man ran a two-hundred-dollar letter of credit past Pope — he was in his
office back there when this Gonzales Mexican
shows up. So Pope gives him a hunnert ninety
on it and Gonzales waits for his drovers,
nursing a damned five-cent glass of suds the
whole hour of it, and then they come in.
Fourteen. And Gonzales slips them each ten
dollars. And then what? Do they whoop and
tree the town and shoot the moon? You tell
me, Sheriff. You toss the usual bunch of
drunks in the calaboose last night?"

"That's why I'm curious, Murphy. It's
never happened before. It can't happen. It's
like the Devil swearing off evil and reforming."

Murphy grinned. "Like an Irishman going
teetotal."

"You got it, Murphy. I'm so amazed, I've
been wondering about it all day. So I came
around to get the story firsthand, just for
the record. The county needs those two-dollar
fines, and I didn't nab a one. What went
wrong?"

"Well now, Sheriff, it happened like this.
Some of those Texans lit out with their money
to buy shirts and boots and all of that —
couple merchants like Horton Gatz stayed
open, just waiting for them to hit town.
This here Gonzales, he spoke soft and gave
each a sort of look. He's a man to give a

look, Sheriff. He gave each one of those weatherbeat rannies a fierce look, and they settled down with a mug of beer apiece, at those tables over there, all together, not mixing around, not sampling Elmer Roderus's faro layout yonder, just setting and sipping."

"Then what?"

"Then nothing! The ones that bought shirts and slickers and knives and cartridges came in and ordered up some suds and sat sipping and talking low. And that segundo, he just sat at the end of the table with balled fists daring any of them to hoot or howl. This went on an hour, and one skinny one they called Corkscrew got mad and started a little hoedown with Gonzales, but fast as this kid stood up, the ranny next to him lifted the kid's six-gun right out of the socket, and then the kid really got mad. But they hushed him down, like they didn't want no one here to know what the outfit was up to. Then, after an hour or so, this Gonzales says, 'Time to go, boys,' and they all troop out and onto their ponies and ride off like deacons."

"What did you make of it, Murphy?"

"I'll tell you what I made of it, Sheriff. That segundo didn't want no gabby drunks or fights or big talk or treeing the town. Like they all had some secret and didn't want it spilled in the good times after a long drive. And the funny thing is, they all went along with it, excepting that skinny proddy kid."

"Any idea what they were hiding, Murphy? Anyone say anything and then get hushed and back off?"

"Well, they talked some about the owner, Bragg, going under and you looking after him. They talked about getting the longhorns up to the Judith country and what they'd find there — nothing, they figured. They talked about those three injured you got in the jail — three Mex I hear — and that's when Gonzales sort of shut 'em down. Oh, yeah, one did say it looked funny that all three injured were Mexican, and another said that was just coincidence, it just happened that way. That's when Gonzales said for them to shut their faces. They was hit by Sioux, that right, Sheriff?"

"Seems to be right, Murphy."

"Oh, yeah, Sheriff. One guy, he says they deserved what they got."

"The Mexicans deserved to be shot?"

"No, the outfit. This Bragg outfit. This one said they deserved it and got away light."

"Who said that? You remember him?"

"Sure, a big, black-haired, baggy-eyed one with shoulders wide as an axe handle. Too

85

big for a cowboy. I'm thinking maybe the cookie in that outfit. Older, too."

"Then what?"

"Gonzales hissed at him, like shut up or something. Then they pulled out fast and that was it. That answer your questions?"

"It makes me even more curious, Murphy. Thanks for your help. If you recollect anything more, you know where to find me."

Santiago left four bits on the counter. Murphy stared, wiped a hand over his center-parted black hair, and nodded.

Chapter 6

The burying of old Iturbide ran only ten minutes. Santiago attended, not only to pay his last respects to a patient, but also to see who might be there. As he walked up the long, steep road to the cemetery on the bluff, he swiftly surveyed those who walked with him behind Sylvane Tobias's fancy new hearse, which was pulled by the black horse. Most of Bragg's outfit, he thought. Anglo and Mexican. Several were absent because of day herding, and Athena Bragg had not come.

Tobias had managed to get a hole dug, but in the farthest corner of the Miles cemetery, a lonely, sagebrush-dotted place. Santiago seethed at the mortician. Old Iturbide was Mexican and a cowpuncher, and that had been enough for Sylvane to consign him to one of the outer circles of hell.

Jefferson Gonzales did the honors, pronouncing Iturbide a fine cow hand and a good man.

"We're close to where we're going now, and if we stick together for this last drive, our friend won't have died in vain," he said quietly. "We'll deliver the Bragg cattle just as we signed on to do, and we'll stay loyal to the brand to our last breath. If we stick together, we'll get Apollo and Miss Athena settled, and then those who want to head south can do so."

Santiago sensed a vague warning and message in the words, but he had no inkling of what it might be. In his pocket was a telegram that Neven had delivered that morning. The sheriff at Uvalde had wired that Bragg had been a prominent man with no criminal record but was thought to have thrown a wide loop getting started and had a reputation for abrasiveness toward his neighbors.

That had confirmed something in Santiago's mind. Disease and fever may have changed Bragg in some ways, bringing out traits he had kept more or less under control in Texas.

Jefferson Gonzales ended with a brief prayer and a request that these men dig into their britches and pay Tobias. Santiago watched closely. If some didn't dig into their pockets, it might be evidence of a quarrel or fight of some kind in the outfit. But the Anglo hands dug into their jeans as readily as the few Mexicans, and soon Tobias had his fifty dollars. Tobias clambered aboard his black vehicle and drove slowly down the hill, while the Bragg cowboys lingered in the quiet morning. Gonzales looked at Santiago expectantly, but Santiago had resolved not to do anything until noon.

"I'll ride out to your camp in a while, Gonzales," he said brusquely.

The drovers walked awkwardly down the slope in their high boots, hating every step taken on their own legs. Their ponies had all been tied to hitch rails along Main Street.

"Apollo," he said, catching up with the boy. "Let's go visit your father. I'm afraid he's worse this morning, lad, and I think you'll want to be with him."

The boy peered up at him sullenly and said nothing.

"I'm sure your father loves you, lad. Maybe it's time for you to tell him that, too."

"Aw, he'll just bawl me out," the boy said miserably. But he followed Santiago anyway as they picked their way down the prairie slope.

"You came to say good-bye to Iturbide, but your sister didn't."

"I'm not supposed to, but I did anyway."

"Why not? Iturbide was a good hand, I gather, and part of the Bragg outfit for a long time. I bet he worked for your father since before you were born."

"Braggs aren't supposed to. She didn't want me to."

Santiago waited for more, but the tanned, slim boy lapsed into troubled silence. Santiago sensed something heavy on the boy, something clamped in and held down by the iron command of elders.

"Your father named you well," Santiago said almost aimlessly. "Apollo was the Greek god of herds and flocks, and here you are, looking over a large herd. He was the god of moral and ethical matters, too, so I guess you'll be making sure that you and your sister will always do what's right."

"I hate my name. My mom hated it, too, but I was stuck with it. Who wants to be named Apollo?"

"Is your mother in Texas?"

"San Antonio."

"Do you ever see her?"

"No Bragg sees her. Father put her out of the house, and she's no good."

The boy's raw tone put a stop to that sort of talk, so Santiago walked quietly awhile, saying nothing.

"Is my father going to die?"

"It's in the hands of God now, Apollo."

"You didn't give me a direct answer. Braggs always insist on direct answers."

"Do you answer the same way, lad?"

"No. I'm not a hired person."

The reply surprised Santiago. "Very well

then, I'm not sure your father will live through this day. He's strong, though, and might linger a while. A few days, a week . . . Now I'll ask you something. You're almost orphaned but not quite. You could go back to Texas and your mother. Or go on up to the Judith country. You're almost a man, lad, but not quite. How will you and your sister manage alone up there?"

"Jefferson."

"Is that your father's wish?"

"It's his order."

"Is it your wish? A wilderness cabin, no father or mother, just your sister with you and some loyal men?"

"I'm a Bragg."

"You ducked my question, lad. Is it your wish? I'm not asking about your father's wishes or orders."

"It's what I got to do," the boy snapped.

They reached the bottom of the slope and trod the dusty path toward town. Ahead of them the drovers hurried on, eager to collect their horses.

"If you were in my shoes now, lad, would you let the Bragg outfit go? You're the sheriff, and you've got to make a choice."

"You're costing us money, holding us."

"Yes, I'm doing that. And pushing you toward the cold weather, too. It troubles me. But when bullets fly, a sheriff has to ask questions. Iturbide was murdered, you know. A bullet killed him. It's my duty to find out who did it and arrest that person for trial."

"Some Sioux."

"Could you identify them, lad?"

"Sure. They weren't like no Injuns I ever seen. They dressed like us — like drovers. Boots and spurs and chapaderos and lariats on their saddles. They were Injuns because they had two black braids coming from under their hats and looked Injun."

"You got a close look?"

"Sure, they came up to talk."

"What was the talk about, Apollo?"

"Just talk."

The boy clammed up suddenly.

"Did they have something to complain about, lad? Had your outfit done something to them they didn't like?"

"I'm a Bragg, Sheriff."

"That's right, Apollo. I wired the sheriff at Uvalde, man named Aaron Bates — I bet you know him. I asked him about you Braggs. He wired back that your father's a tough man but hasn't any known record of wrongdoing. He said maybe your dad mavericked a lot of calves to get started, but that was only talk."

"He should mind his own business, and so should you!"

"I got a murder on my hands, Apollo. And I got a young man beside me named after the Greek god of ethics and morals. So I'm counting on you to live up to both names you got. Being Bragg — and being Apollo."

"Athena'd kill me. Pa would, too."

"You came up pretty close to Pine Ridge Reservation, down near the corner of Dakota, didn't you?"

The boy nodded.

"You think maybe those Sioux in cowboy duds, those Sioux that looked to be cowpunchers living as white men do — maybe they had something to do with that new Sioux beef herd there?"

The boy said nothing and looked miserable.

They entered Miles, walking up saloon row on Park Street and toward the center of town. The drovers had collected their horses and scattered. They trudged past Tobias's place, and Santiago glimpsed the man back at his carriage shed stripping harness off the black horse.

"Your men chipped in and gave old Iturbide a good funeral. It looked to me like they were all fond of the old man and loyal to him. You got Mexicans and Anglos in your outfit, and they get along pretty well, I'd say, lad."

"Pa made sure of it! I saw him knock out some smart alec from Austin with one punch because he got to riding the Mex. Pa says the Mex are his best hands, know the stock better, got more skills than any dozen Texans. He got rid of that one."

"Sounds like your pa's a good man and knew good men."

"He does!"

He steered the boy through the gate in his picket fence and around the side of his cottage toward the summer kitchen at the rear. Mimi no doubt saw them. She saw everything, Indian-fashion. He slid a hand over the boy's shoulder.

"Your father's back here, son. Best we could do."

They slipped through the door and into the cool shade of the summer kitchen. From the cot rose the sound of hoarse, irregular breathing. The boy seemed reluctant to approach, but Santiago slid a comforting arm about his shoulders.

"Mr. Bragg, I've brought your son to you."

Slowly Bragg opened his eyes — burning coals in a gaunt, wasted face.

"Apollo wants to tell you he'll carry on as best as he knows how, sir."

Bragg tried to say something, only to convulse with coughing again. When it subsided, he spoke. "Get the hell out," he muttered. "Kid should be pushing the herd."

Santiago waited. The boy trembled, and tears slid down his brown cheeks.

"Your pa has a fever, lad, and isn't talking the way he should. Would you like to say anything to him? That you love him and wish him all the goodness in the universe?"

The boy shivered and began sobbing softly, overwhelmed by the sight of his dying father.

"It's true, Pa! It's true. I always loved you."

"Go to hell," muttered Hermes Bragg.

The boy peered up at Santiago with helpless, miserable eyes.

"Tell him how you feel, lad, and then we'll say goodbye."

"Pa . . . Pa . . ." But Apollo could manage no more.

Santiago led him quietly into the kitchen where Mimi waited with tea and cookies.

Santiago found the drovers in Bragg's cow camp packed up and ready to go. Miss Athena sat irritably on the seat of the covered wagon, waiting. Half the drovers had left, riding out to drag and flank positions. The cavvy had been gathered and run in with the cattle, which bawled restlessly on earth stripped bare.

He'd ridden back with Apollo, mulling the things he'd learned from the boy, and wondering how to deliver the bad news to Jefferson Gonzales.

"Are we free now, Sheriff?" asked the segundo.

"I'm afraid not, Gonzales. There's one last task. I want you to run the beeves past me in bunches so I can read the brands."

"Why the hell do we have to do that?" exploded Gonzales.

Santiago didn't answer. Apollo looked stricken.

"We're leaving," snapped the girl.

"Not for a little while, Miss Bragg."

"The hell with you! We're moving out!" She waved at her crew. "Start 'em up."

"Checking brands would take the rest of the day. You told us noon!" Gonzales said.

"Sorry. Have your men cut out around twenty and walk them past me, Mr. Gonzales."

"And if we don't?"

"You go nowhere."

"Would you mind telling me why?"

"New information."

Santiago glanced at young Apollo, who sat his mount with dread written on his face.

96

"Sheriff at Uvalde says Hermes Bragg was a little free with his lariat."

Something relaxed slightly in Gonzales's glare.

"Well, if that's all it is, I can straighten it out. Miss Athena has sales papers on rebranded animals. The rest have our brand. Would the papers do?"

"No, Mr. Gonzales."

"You want a cut? You want a toll fee? How many beeves?"

"You misread me, Mr. Gonzales. Now let's get on with the brand inspection. Tell me, when did you leave Uvalde?"

"Late April."

"And you road-branded just before you left?"

Gonzales nodded reluctantly.

"Get going!" yelled Athena. "Get going!" She cracked the lines over the croups of her team, and her wagon lurched forward. Santiago ignored her.

"Mr. Gonzales, I noticed a couple of pretty fresh road brands when I rode through the herd the other day."

"Sure! Happens all the time. We run into strays. We collected some south of the Red River. You can't keep them out. They want to join the rest. You cut them out — it takes a lot of time and effort — and next thing they're back in. So what you do is note the brands and pay the owners when the cattle are shipped to the stockyards. That's so commonplace I think you don't know much about trailing beef. We lost a lot — maybe ten percent — because of some bad river crossings, one stampede, and a bad lightning storm. Picked up a few we got to pay for."

Santiago grinned. "Now you'll have a chance to count 'em."

"You're holding us to it? How about if me and you ride in and look? I can show you three, four of those that got sucked in."

A hundred yards ahead the covered wagon halted. Athena slowly turned it around and returned because no one had followed her.

"I'd like to think you're not hiding something, Mr. Gonzales. If you drive the beeves past me the way I said, I'll take it that you're not hiding anything from me."

Gonzales said nothing as they watched Athena drive back, her face a thundercloud. She stopped twenty feet from them.

"Is he keeping us here?" she asked Gonzales.

The segundo nodded.

"This is a free country! You got no right!"

"One of your men lies in a fresh grave, shot to death. Two others are seriously injured, Miss Bragg."

"We get hurt and you blame us!"

Santiago sighed. "Mr. Gonzales, I'm going to ride through your herd. It won't be a short ride. I intend to look at every beeve you've got. It's going to take longer than if you cooperated."

He touched heels to his big bay, St. James, and the horse sprang into a fast walk.

"Stop!" she cried.

Santiago turned. Leveled at his back was a double-bore shotgun. She peered down its barrel at him.

"Lift your hands!"

He didn't.

She lifted the barrel slightly and fired. The blast rocketed through the quiet afternoon. He felt a rush of air just over his head. Slowly, in fear of his life, he lifted his hands.

"You're in trouble, miss," he managed to mutter.

"I'm a Bragg. Gonzales, pull his gun."

"You're in trouble, too, Gonzales."

The segundo peered starkly at the dark barrel that could swing inches and catch him and reluctantly reined close to Santiago. He pulled the sheriff's revolver from its black holster.

"Start for Miles, Sheriff. If you follow

us, you're dead." She wiggled the shotgun for emphasis.

He thought better than to argue. She shoved a new shell into the barrel she'd fired. He sat stock-still, unwilling to move himself or his horse.

"You heard me, Sheriff."

He lowered his hands slowly, collected the reins dangling from the bridle to the ground, and started walking, half expecting a load of buckshot in his back and afraid for his life. Each ticking second seemed likely to be his last. But the girl didn't shoot.

"Apollo. What did you tell him?" she roared.

The boy didn't answer.

Santiago took a chance. "He told me the Indians who attacked you were herders in cowpunching duds, chapaderos, and that they had a little talk with you before the fight, Miss Bragg."

She looked at Apollo, enraged.

"What'd you tell him lies like that for?"

The boy looked torn, but suddenly he sat straight in his saddle. "I didn't lie, Athena," he said fiercely. "I'm Apollo Bragg."

"You're not a Bragg. You're just a lying yellow dog!"

"You did the right thing, lad."

She replied to that with another blast of

the shotgun. It set the cattle to trotting, a giant wave of movement behind them.

The sudden pulse of the hungry herd energized the whole crew, and the quiet afternoon exploded into yips and yelps of cowpunchers prodding two thousand beeves into a moving mass of animals.

Around Santiago wagons clattered to life. The cookie on the chuck wagon snapped the lines to his mules. The cavvy wrangler whipped his drays into motion. A rising thunder told of a trail herd marching north once again. The unarmed sheriff watched it all, chagrined that a slip of a girl had disarmed and thwarted him, a girl ready to kill him for whatever twisted reasons lay in her brain.

North? thought Santiago. The Yellowstone River lay just north of them, and somewhere they'd have to cross it, swimming its wide torrent and swift current if they hoped to head north. They weren't going anywhere he couldn't catch them in the next day or so. Weary and disappointed with himself, he reined his bay toward Miles. He'd been humbled as a doctor, helpless before the onslaught of death. But never as a sheriff had he been so humbled, and by a fourteen-year-old girl named Athena Bragg.

Chapter 7

Santiago tied the bay to the hitch rail outside of his barn and walked wearily into his house, glancing at Bragg as he passed. The cattleman breathed quietly.

Mimi looked at him sharply. "Santo, what's wrong?"

"I was just bested by a girl with a shotgun."

He was lucky to be alive, he thought. That girl would have fired a barrel at him for any reason. Some sheriff, he thought, feeling chagrined.

Mimi laughed. No sympathy at all.

"She fired at me, Mimi. Buckshot missed my head by inches."

"Oh, Santo!" She looked stricken. "When you go away on sheriff things, I wonder if you'll come home."

"So do I. Any patients waiting?"

"No."

He pushed into his offices and pulled his spare revolver, an old Starr confiscated from a cowboy, out of a drawer. From wall brackets he grabbed his sawed-off shotgun and checked the loads.

"Santo! What are you doing?"

"Going after that girl."

"Is that wise?"

"It's law."

"What are you going to do with her? Surely not throw her in jail."

"A day in jail might teach a fourteen-year-old snip a lesson, Mimi."

"But Santo — she commands armed men. Are you sure?"

"I do what I have to. I don't enforce the law selectively, let this one go, arrest that one."

"But — she's just a girl."

"She's a Bragg."

He had what he needed. Spare loads for the Starr, the shotgun, and a pair of manacles.

"You're going to lock the girl in those?"

"Yes, I intend to."

"And you'll ride back to town with the girl in manacles, down Main Street for all to see."

He didn't answer. Mimi followed him through the quiet house, past the sleeping man in the summer kitchen, and out to the bay, watching silently as he slid the shotgun into a sheath and mounted.

"Take a posse, Santo."

"This is my little war, Mimi."

"You'll do something you'll regret," she said bitterly, as he mounted and steered the bay west.

He rode quietly down Main Street, noting a few ranch wagons in front of J. J. Graham's hardware and little else on a quiet summer afternoon. The sun's heat caught in his black frock coat and trousers, warming them. He crossed the Tongue River bridge, his horse's shod hoofs echoing hollowly on the heavy planks.

The herd had headed up the Tongue and west, along the Northern Pacific right of way and under the nose of Fort Keogh. Jefferson Gonzales wouldn't much like running a herd along the railroad and would try to cross as soon as he could. The south side of the river would be heavily grazed by cavalry mounts anyway.

After that, what? West up the Yellowstone, he thought. Probably to Horse Creek, or more likely, Froze to Death Creek, and over the low divide to the big bend of the Musselshell and then westward up it to Judith Gap. It wouldn't be hard to track over two thousand beeves, he thought.

He picked up the trail easily and followed the broad band of pummeled bunchgrass and torn earth and cowflops westward along the shining rails. The drovers had made some effort to keep the herd off the tracks and crowded toward the south bluffs. He hunted in vain for wheel tracks and found none, which meant that the wagons ranged ahead of the herd, ahead of the dust and grit. Above and out of sight from the river valley loomed Fort Keogh. He rode over the military reservation and saw that the herd had crossed its eastern boundary near the Northern Pacific right-of-way. He wondered if the officers knew or cared.

The river cut through steep, grassy hills that sometimes shouldered so close to the water that there was room only for the railroad and no bottoms at all. There the herd had been driven directly up the track or along a wagon road right beside it. They'd made time, no doubt about it, with that girl and Gonzales hurrying to get as far from Miles and the law as possible. But he was making faster time on a bay with an easy jog, and occasionally he glimpsed the golden glow of trail dust ahead or caught the faint roll of bawling cattle on the breeze.

A little west of Keogh he rounded a shoulder and discovered the herd ahead, stopped dead and milling while drovers penned it. A lot of animals had drifted to the river, plowed through brush, and were watering. The track was covered with animals, and the rails looked slick with green manure.

Puzzled, Santiago rode past the drovers at the drag, most of them with bandannas over

105

their noses, sitting quietly on their scrawny Texas ponies. He pushed through milling cattle, ducking around knots of them and detouring around feisty longhorns that looked ready to make trouble. The middle of the herd seemed almost a golden haze to him, and he noted that the north shore of the river seemed dim and blurred in the dust.

It seemed a good chance to examine brands, so he watched sharply as he threaded through the massed cattle. The HB road brand had been burned into left shoulders, and he saw nothing amiss. These brands had been burned in months ago. April, Gonzales had said. Toole's bay thoroughbred, no cattle horse at all, didn't like this journey through the dense herd and grew nervous under him, startling easily and tossing his head and finally mincing, ready to explode. Santiago pulled him down to a quiet walk and pushed forward.

Then suddenly he almost bumped into a freshly branded animal. He pulled back his reins and studied the big brindle longhorn. Not so fresh at that, he thought. The flesh had long since healed over but lay white and hairless, unlike the haired-over older brands. From his saddle he studied the big cow, looking for another brand, gradually circling the animal. Why did this cow have

106

a fresh HB on the shoulder? He reined in close and felt his nervous bay resist every step, wanting to stay clear of those sweeping horns. The brand wasn't right. He saw signs of tampering, parts of the H new and part old. The cow decided she didn't like being examined and trotted away, her head turned back toward Santiago. But he'd seen enough.

Theft. He had a question or two to ask at the fort before he knew that for sure. He pushed forward again, wondering how he'd handle the matter. He didn't expect a dozen-and-a-half drovers and the Bragg children to surrender easily to a lone sheriff. He pushed ahead, feeling deeply disappointed. Jefferson Gonzales had struck him as an honorable man. Even the Bragg children had struck him as people who knew better than to steal. And the drovers didn't look like hardcases at all, just another bunch of Texas cowpunchers, wild and woolly but basically honest.

The bottoms widened, and he steered to the edge of the herd where he could make better time. A sadness settled through him as he sensed the end of all this. He hated to think of the future and the things he'd have to do. Hated to think of what it would mean to Apollo and Miss Athena. He reached the edge of the herd and rode along the slopes of the river bluff, keeping a sharp eye out for more recently branded critters. He spotted several. Ahead and around a headland he spotted the tops of the wagons and rode warily toward them, wondering what to do. He decided on caution. He needed one confirming piece of evidence from Fort Keogh. And he needed a posse. This trip would be for Athena, if he could get her.

He wasn't surprised to discover blue-coated soldiers around the wagons. Even from a distance he could see the gold-threaded epaulets of officers among them; he knew the army had come to meddle. It always did. Colonel Wade had a habit of making everything his business, whether civilian or military.

Santiago could see that the Bragg boy and girl and Gonzales were engaged in heated talk with officers as he rode in. Several drovers sat loosely on their ponies, among them that young menace Corkscrew, who had new Miles City grips on his battered revolver. The sheriff rode up quietly, while soldiers and drovers glared at him. Neither side welcomed his presence a bit, he thought. He spotted the commanding officer, a captain, several sergeants, and a dozen enlisted men in the crowd.

"It's you," said Colonel Wade.

Athena Bragg glared at him.

"What's all this about?" asked Santiago.

"None of your business!" snapped the girl.

"They're trying to cross the military reservation, and I'm saying no. They can go around, like the other herds. This is cavalry grass."

"All we want to do is cross."

"These are our best bottoms. We're always short of feed, and we cut a lot of hay here. Sorry, Miss Bragg."

She turned fiercely toward Santiago. "You should have told us!"

Santiago laughed easily. "I believe you were driving me away at gunpoint when your herd started running, Miss Bragg."

She turned to Wade. "I'm Athena Bragg, and I'll see you cashiered if you don't let us through."

Wade sighed. "Captain, direct the squad to shoot any beeves that cross into the hay meadows."

The captain hustled off and began barking orders. Soldiers trotted out into a line in front of the herd and rammed cartridges into the chambers of their Springfields.

Santiago sighed. The fort had always guarded its hay bottoms zealously. Other trail herds had been directed around them, either well west or to the east of Miles City.

"I think, Miss Bragg, you'd better turn the herd around. I'll show you to a fresh bedding ground a little east of town. Then I want you and your brother and your segundo here, Mr. Gonzales, to come with me."

"What for?"

"Oh, shooting at a sheriff, disarming a sheriff, resisting a lawful investigation, and anything more I can toss at you."

Wade's eyes widened. "What's all this about, Toole?"

"Civilian matter, Colonel."

"This is about that shooting scrape these people had with the Sioux?"

"I'd say so."

"Then it's army business, Toole."

That's the way it'd always been, Santiago thought irritably. The army bullied in on nearly every investigation he undertook. Half the time he rounded up drunken or violent soldiers in Miles City, the army thwarted civilian justice. It rankled him.

He ignored Wade. Let the man bluster. "Mr. Gonzales," he said. "You owe me a revolver."

Silently the segundo unbuckled a saddlebag and pulled out Santiago's black Remington and handed it to Toole.

"I did what I had to, Sheriff. She was

110

pointing that shotgun at me."

"Sorry, I don't buy that. You knew well enough she'd never shoot her right-hand man. No, Mr. Gonzales, you disarmed me because she told you to and never in your life have you questioned a Bragg. Even when she asked you to defy the law. I'm taking you before the magistrate, too."

Jefferson Gonzales looked humiliated, and Santiago felt some small pity for him. A good man probably but full of blind obedience.

"What's all this about?" demanded Colonel Wade.

But his question was obscured by a low rumble and a long, sad wail rising from the west.

"A train! And cattle all over the tracks," snapped Gonzales.

He wheeled off to help his drovers even as the angry wail of the chuffing locomotive loomed louder under the overcast sky. Cattle bawled restlessly, terrified by the train's noise. Then, in a flash, the animals began trotting east, turning themselves into a lithe, sinuous cascade of trotting cattle escaping the hiss and chuff and screeching brakes of the eastbound train.

"Stampede!" cried Apollo. He lashed the mules pulling the Bragg wagon toward the slopes of the bluffs. Soldiers began dashing toward the high ground until they realized the herd had turned and was thundering east, toward Miles, to escape the freight train now squealing down on locked wheels to avoid ramming a sea of beeves. Whooping drovers yelling Texas profanities slowly pushed the herd south of the rails. But several beeves had caught their hoofs in the ties and lay broken and struggling on the right-of-way. The cowcatcher of the engine smacked violently into one, pitching it to the right and killing it instantly. Santiago surveyed the situation swiftly and decided he and the others were in no danger. This train drove the herd east. A westbound train would have stampeded the cattle right over them all.

"Now look what you've done!" yelled Athena Bragg to everyone and no one. "Killed my beeves!"

Santiago came to a swift decision. "Miss Bragg," he said softly, "you and Apollo follow me to town in that wagon. I'm holding you on charges."

"You can't do this! I'm a Bragg!"

"Braggs aren't above the law. Not even female Braggs. Now you come along or I'll take you along."

She glared ferociously and glanced at the shotgun lying on the floorboards.

"Come on, Athena, the herd's going that

112

way anyhow," Apollo said gently. She snarled imperiously at him, but he held the lines and swung the mule team around. The small freight squealed by, slowing to a halt while cattle bolted pell-mell out of its path.

"Toole! Where are you going?" yelled Wade.

Santiago ignored him.

Apollo drove the covered wagon slowly toward Miles City with swift, apologetic glances toward Sheriff Toole, who rode nearby, keeping a sharp watch on the dagger-eyed girl.

"Miss Bragg, slowly lift that shotgun at your feet and hand it to me butt first." Santiago crowded close to the seat, ready to land on her if she turned reckless, but she obeyed sullenly with a kind of imperious attitude that made him smile. He marveled at her, at her untrammeled will and uninhibited ferocity. He'd never come across a young lady like that. He slid her shotgun across his lap and grinned. She spat at him.

"Texas manners?"

She spat at him again.

As they rolled slowly to town, he decided to go ahead and bring charges. The girl had a lesson to learn, and a twenty-five dollar fine plus a day in the pokey imposed by the justice of the peace, Pericles Shaw, might bulldog her.

Far ahead the drovers had wheeled the herd directly into the Tongue River, where animals halted, bawled, slurped water, and turned the flow green. Good, he thought. Gonzales would cool them down and then drive them to fresh bedground east of town a few miles. He sensed that the segundo would get his drovers organized and then ride to town and turn himself in. The man had grit and courage.

Apollo followed Santiago across the Tongue bridge and on into Miles, straight down Main Street toward the sandstone jail. At a nod from the sheriff, the boy halted the wagon, looking frightened. Even Athena seemed more subdued than enraged, he thought. Good enough.

He beckoned them in, filled out a form, and walked the seething girl to a rear cell, past the two injured Bragg men, who watched silently. The clang of the closing cell door echoed, and the girl stood behind bars, sullen and at last afraid.

"Big tough sheriff, picking on women," she jeered at last. Her voice seemed oddly small and lost in the hard rock cellroom.

In his office young Apollo waited miserably, choking back tears.

"I'll be with you in a moment, lad. While I'm here I'll look after our two patients.

They're men your father disowns. He suggested I shoot them. Do you agree?"

The boy shook his head slowly.

"Give me a direct answer, son."

"I'm a Bragg," he said defiantly.

Santiago plucked up his Gladstone and checked on his patients. The one with the shot-out cheek looked better. He'd have a ghastly scar that'd disfigure his face, and no doubt eating problems. The other man, sallow and sweating, ran a raging fever. His right lung sounded congested. His wounded leg lay hot and swollen, with ugly purple streaks sunraying from the bullet wound. Too late for amputation, Santiago thought. The man would either conquer his infections and pneumonia or not. And the doctor had scarcely a drug in his arsenal of powders to help.

"*Malo,*" the man muttered.

Santiago agreed. He saw Athena staring from her cell across the corridor. "This man is suffering for you. He may not make it," Santiago said to her. She jerked her gaze elsewhere with a toss of her head.

"Think it over, young lady. One man's given his life for you. This one may also. Are you worth it?"

She turned and glared at him with unblinking gray eyes.

He pocketed the cell key this time, now

that he had a prisoner. Apollo watched quietly, his face somber with fear.

"Apollo, lad. You were a witness. Have you the courage to write a statement of what you saw your sister do? Or testify to it before the justice of the peace?"

The boy looked tormented and then straightened up, finding some inner strength. "If I do, will you release her?"

"I can't speak for the magistrate, lad. But I suppose he will fine her and release her tomorrow. But shooting at a sheriff is a serious thing."

"I know."

"You think about doing what's right, Apollo Bragg."

The boy looked crushed by a load too heavy for any twelve-year-old.

"You're not a prisoner, lad. You can stay here in town or out at your cow camp. Your wagon's here. You can bring it to my house and stay in town, close to Athena and your father. I think Jefferson Gonzales will be along soon. He faces charges, too, lad, and I'm guessing he has the courage to come to me."

"I'll wait for him," the boy said. "I don't want to stay here, and I don't want to be around my father."

"I'm going to walk my afternoon rounds,

116

Apollo. Would you like to come along? I'd enjoy the company."

"You would?" The slim boy stood and waited, while Santiago set his Gladstone bag aside and slid his recovered Remington back into its holster.

Santiago had the distinct feeling the boy ached to say something. He slipped an arm over Apollo's shoulder and steered him out onto Main Street.

Chapter 8

The overnight change in Hermes Bragg astonished Santiago. The big man lay quietly on his cot staring soberly up at the doctor. The febrile wildness had receded. His forehead felt cooler. Santiago's stethoscope revealed a steady, slower pulse, but the man's lungs remained a rumbling ruin. Somehow the husk of the man's powerful body had rallied, but it was only a stay of execution.

"You're looking better this morning."

"Am I going to live?"

"That's in the hands of God, Mr. Bragg."

"You're not giving me a direct answer."

Santiago shrugged. "You've won a respite. I don't know how long it'll last. Your lungs are destroyed."

"Why am I better?"

"The human body has resources that are the marvel of all doctors, sir. We don't know how it conquers fevers and fights disease, but it does. In your case, this bed rest certainly helps. And just as importantly you aren't breathing the trail dust of your herd each day, with its alkali and bits of manure and other things that can inflame your weakened lungs."

"But the consumption will take me?"

"I'm sorry, sir. I see little hope in the long run."

Bragg hoisted himself up on an elbow. "Would you give me a year, Toole?"

"I can't make such predictions. Your sole hope is to stay here in Miles and in bed, in a comfortable warm place without drafts. That and a good diet: fruits, vegetables, meats, grains. I'll tell you this: if you attempt to survive in a drafty cabin in the Judith wilderness, far away from sources of good food, you won't last a minute."

While he talked, Santiago prepared a draught of white vitriol for the cattleman to gargle. It would help the ulcerations on his larynx.

"Gargle this. Don't swallow."

But Bragg proved to be too weak to sit up. He coughed spastically.

"What does that stuff do?"

"It kills germs in your throat."

"Germs? What's that?"

Santiago sighed. He'd encountered this over and over in North America. No one — even doctors — knew about germs, bacteria, Pasteur, Lister, and Koch, who'd recently isolated the tuberculosis bacillus.

"Germs are tiny organisms invisible to the naked eye but observable with a microscope. They cause infections. We know how to kill

119

them on the surface of the body and elsewhere with antiseptics such as carbolic. We don't know how to deal with them inside the body, where they do harm. We've known how they infect the human body since the sixties."

"My Texas docs said I got consumption from miasmas in the damp air."

Toole said nothing.

"I don't reckon as I believe you," Bragg added. "A lot of bull, that's what it is."

Santiago shrugged. He'd fought this fight many times. Some day the world would understand. But an old guard of medical practitioners hooted at the whole idea — and killed off patients regularly by refusing even to experiment with antiseptic methods.

"I'll leave that white vitriol here. When you're able to sit up and gargle, do it."

Bragg sagged back on his cot, exhausted. "Where's my herd?" he demanded.

"On a bedground east of town, I believe."

"You still holding it?"

"No. But I'm holding your daughter for shooting at me, and I'll bring charges against Jefferson Gonzales for disarming me and obstructing an investigation."

"What! Where is she?"

"The Miles City jail."

"You can't do that! I'll have you cashiered, Toole."

"That's what your daughter was saying. One of you's a parrot. Get total rest now or you'll slide back into trouble."

"What investigation?"

"Of fresh road brands on cattle in your herd. Want to talk about it, Bragg?"

The cattleman glared sullenly. "If I had my strength, I'd whip you to a pulp, Toole."

"That's what I like about you, Bragg. I always know where I stand with you."

A new paroxysm of coughing convulsed Bragg, and he settled back under his blankets with hopelessness written across his face.

"If you want to live, rest now," Santiago said.

He left, feeling the conflict between his sheriff duties and his medical nurturing. He hiked briskly to his sheriff's office and jail, intending to arraign Athena Bragg. When he reached his bailiwick there was a Bragg cowpony at the hitch rail and he found Jefferson Gonzales slouched in a chair waiting for him.

Santiago grunted. "I was giving up hope on you."

"I'll take my medicine, Sheriff. It took all evening to get the herd settled on decent grass. About half my drovers are ready to quit me, and the other half are unhappy or angry or full of fight and wanting to tear

121

up the town — "

"I'm dropping the charge, Mr. Gonzales. You came in. I wanted to make the point with you that blind obedience to a command from a Bragg is no excuse for lawless conduct. Now I want something from you. I want some frank talk — about the fresh road brands, about what happened down around Fort Robinson. And I want your cooperation when I examine that herd this morning."

Gonzales slid into silence, looking trapped.

"Think about it. And while you're thinking, I'd like you along with me. I'm taking Miss Athena to the justice of the peace in the building next door. If you want a lawyer for her, get one. I'm going to have the county attorney subpoena you as a witness. You saw her shoot at me." He eyed the nervous segundo. "Or, if you want to get it over with fast, you can tell the magistrate what you saw and she can plead guilty, take her medicine, and get out. I think the JP, Pericles Shaw, will settle for about fifty dollars and the night in jail she's already served. Fifty dollars is a cheap price for an attempt on my life, Mr. Gonzales."

Gonzales grinned. "You've got me treed," he said, and laughed amiably.

"The boy, Apollo, saw it, too. I thought of subpoenaing him to testify against his sister but thought better of it. Too much for a lad. He's a good boy. We had a little talk last night. He walked my rounds with me. He was bursting to tell me something but didn't, and I didn't press him. Mr. Gonzales, I've never seen a lad in such a corner. His father's crushed him. His sister torments him. But something inside the boy runs true. He's got a guilty secret, and it's a millstone. All the Braggs have a guilty secret. And so do you, Mr. Gonzales, so do you."

Gonzales peered somberly out the window. His knotty brown hands worked their way around the brim of the hat they were clutching.

"I reckon you've got a loop over it all," he muttered.

"I think I do. Disease can change a man, isn't it so, Mr. Gonzales? Maybe bring out bad traits that a man's spent a lifetime beating down inside of himself."

Gonzales turned from the light, his face flinty. "Let's get this over with, Sheriff."

Santiago agreed. He unlocked the door to the cellroom, carrying his Gladstone bag. The patients first. Gonzales followed quietly.

"I'm sorry I had to lock the cellroom door, Mr. Gonzales. With a prisoner, things change."

"Gonzales, get me out of here!" screamed

Athena, clutching the bars of her cell. "I hate this place. I hate this stupid city. I hate this *caponera* sheriff. I hate — "

"Miss Athena — " the segundo began.

"I'll get to you shortly, young woman," said Santiago. "Patients come first."

"I come first, you stupid *cabrón*."

"I take it *cabrón*'s a term of endearment, Gonzales?"

The segundo laughed.

"I didn't even have any privacy," she bawled. "My pail stinks. I'm hungry."

All in all, Santiago thought, Athena was coming along quite nicely. He settled down beside Montoya, the one with the bad leg, and studied the man. Montoya brightened at the sight of Gonzales standing in the cell door and smiled weakly.

But the man looked bad. Feverish. His forehead and cheeks glistened with sweat. Great dark hollows bagged his eyes. The rank smell of mortification leaked from the bandage around his thigh. Santiago pressed his stethoscope against the man's chest and listened to air bubble loudly through the congested lung. He felt helpless.

Santiago cut bandaging away from the hot, inflamed thigh. The flesh was so febrile it burned to his touch and so engorged that it swelled around the taut muslin. He'd apply some more permanganate of potash, but it wouldn't help much. The battle was locked in the blood now, the lungs, a brain being fried by fever. He pulled the dressing away and loosed a foul odor that rose from putrescent, mortifying flesh. He examined the mess dourly.

"When I get out of here I'll kill you!" yelled the girl.

Too late, too late, he thought grimly. He cleaned the pus and rotting flesh away, applied more permanganate, and rebandaged the thigh. He could offer this man only sleep and hope that sleep, the greatest medicine, might heal. He poured a maximum dose of tincture of opium, fifteen drops, into a spoon and slid the laudanum down Montoya's throat and waited. Swiftly the man's face softened and his eyes closed.

The other one, José, seemed better. He'd recover. The swelling had gone down. Putrefaction had stopped. He could open his jaw farther. Santiago rinsed the man's mouth with white vitriol and gave him some Dover's Powder as an anodyne if he needed it. Then he checked on Montoya, who'd slid into deep sleep. The doctor dropped all his gear back into his Gladstone bag.

"Bueno," he said to the injured man. José smiled, lopsidedly, from a distorted face.

He strolled over to Athena's cell. "How do you feel about these wounded men of yours, Miss Bragg?"

"Get me out of here."

"One's dead. I don't expect another to live."

"So what?"

"They gave everything for you Braggs."

"That's what they're paid to do."

"Have you no pity, Miss Bragg? No caring?"

"Why should I?"

"Because no one would have died if your father had done what's right."

"I don't know what you're talking about!"

He eyed her malevolently. She needed a week behind bars, not a night. Maybe a month or even six months.

"Very well. I'm taking you now before our justice of the peace, Pericles T. Shaw, for arraignment on several charges, including attempted murder of me."

"I didn't hit you. I lifted the shotgun."

"I'm glad you admit the crime before a witness, Miss Bragg."

"Gonzales? He doesn't count."

Jefferson Gonzales glowered at her. She smirked at him.

"Get me out of here! I can't stand it another minute! A pail for my duties, and dying men all around me — "

Santiago unlocked the cell door and then barred the opening with his body. "Your hands, Miss Bragg. Out in front of you."

She glared and he waited. He stood patiently. Eventually she surrendered and thrust an arm out, which he cuffed at the wrist. He waited for her other arm. Muttering fiercely, she thrust it out, and he cuffed that arm also, then led her out of the building to the small log courtroom next door.

A volley of shots erupted from within, and the girl turned fearfully to Santiago.

"Don't worry, Miss Bragg. His honor likes to shoot flies."

She plainly didn't believe him.

"He loads his six-gun with half a charge of powder and a paper twist of sand," he added. "It sometimes rains sand during a trial."

Another burst of shots punctuated their arrival. On a shellacked plank dais before them sat Pericles Shaw, blasting greenbottle blowflies. The log room boomed with noise.

Shaw peered over half-glasses at Athena, studying her manacles, and set the weapon down, barrel forward and directly upon the prisoner. She gaped at the man. The JP was a man to gape at, Santiago thought. His shiny bald head was rimmed by gray hair over the ears and jowls that hung like sleigh runners on either side of a porky jaw.

"Look what the cat dragged in," he said.

"You can't do this to me!"

"Your Honor, this is Miss Athena Bragg. I'm charging her with shooting at me with a shotgun, resisting arrest, and impeding my investigation for starters. There'll be a few more."

"Go to hell!"

"Tut tut," wheezed Shaw. He grabbed his six-gun by the barrel and banged the butt of it on the planks as a gavel. Several times this maneuver had resulted in the sudden discharge of a load of sand into Shaw's ample gut, which was always protected by a greasy watershot silk maroon vest, but that never slowed him down.

"How plead you, missy?"

"I'm not going to talk. I'm not going to say a word!"

"Guilty then. That'll be sixty days and a hunnert dollars cash money or gold."

"How dare you!"

"Hold still. There's a greenbelly on your boot." He picked up his six-gun, sighted down its barrel, and squeezed.

Just then the fly took off. Shaw released his trigger finger, disappointed.

"I'll get the little cootie," he muttered. "Toole, how come you haven't brought anything in lately? County coffers getting mighty low. If you don't haul in some lowlifes, I'll call it dereliction of duty."

"Well, here's one right here, your honor. She's from Texas."

"I'll kill you, Toole!" she raged.

Shaw banged his six-gun. "Threatening the life of a duly constituted officer of the law. Twenty-five dollars and costs, missy."

"Miss Athena — " began Gonzales, hat in hand.

"Don't you Miss Athena me! I'll kill you all!"

"Thirty dollars and costs."

"Your honor," began Santiago. "I don't think Miss Bragg understood that when she said she wouldn't talk she was pleading nolo contendere. I'd suggest we start this over. Let her obtain counsel if she wishes."

"Burnball's drunk."

"I'd recommend, sir, that you begin over. If Miss Bragg pleads guilty, I think fifty dollars might be appropriate. If she pleads innocent, I'd suggest setting a trial date a week hence and having Stearn subpoena this gent here, Jefferson Gonzales, who witnessed the event, and prepare a proper bill."

Pericles Shaw massacred a fly on the plank ceiling.

"Death to unbelievers," said Shaw, reload-

129

ing the chamber.

"Miss Bragg, there you have it. You can plead guilty and pay the fifty dollars, or innocent and have a trial a week from now. I'll make sure witnesses are subpoenaed. Mr. Gonzales saw it. Your brother saw it. Half your crew saw it."

"They didn't see anything," she snapped.

"How you plead, missy?" Shaw flapped his gums at her.

"Go to hell."

"I've never heard that plea before. Lock her up, Toole. We'll start this ball in a week."

"You mean I got to spend a week in that hole?"

"You just said you wanted to go to hell, missy."

"Miss Bragg," said Santiago. "Perhaps you can get out on bail. By putting up a bond. I'm sure Mr. Gonzales will find counsel for you, and maybe you can come up with some bail money."

"You can't do this! I'm a Bragg! I'm a girl!"

"Laws apply to Braggs and girls, I'm afraid."

"Bond'll be five thousand. Capital felonious assault and assorted misdemeanors," rasped the magistrate.

Shaw was zeroing in on a big black horsefly, and Santiago scurried back, pulling the girl with him. They reached the door before an explosion punctuated their exit.

"I hate you all," she said, beginning to weep. "We don't have cash for a bond."

Jefferson Gonzales looked gray with weariness. Santiago returned Athena to her cell and freed her wrists. He walked on out to the office with the clang of the cell door in his ears.

"I'm sorry, Mr. Gonzales," he said softly. "It's hard on her. This isn't south Texas, and she has no privileges here."

"He's a rough hombre."

"A diamond in the rough, actually. Strangely enough, justice gets done, give or take a thumb on the guilty scale to keep the county coffers full."

Gonzales laughed softly. "I think it's your design to let her stew in there."

"I wish it could be otherwise. I wish I could send you all on your way. You need time to build shelter and corrals up on the Judith before winter blows in. The next thing'll be hard, Mr. Gonzales. It is going to tear you to pieces, tug at your lifelong loyalties to the Braggs, rip your crew to bits."

That caught the segundo's ear.

"I'd like to examine your herd now, and I'd like your help. Otherwise I'll have to recruit help from the army, which I'd rather avoid. They've a heavy-handed way of doing things. If I find what I expect to find, I think I can deal with it a little better. They'll have some interest. Scrapes with Indians are their business. I don't have jurisdiction over anything that happened in the southwest corner of Dakota, in the vicinity of Pine Ridge. I may have jurisdiction over a fight that happened down on the Little Powder."

Gonzales stared at him stonily.

"You see, sir, I think Hermes Bragg was a good man once. You're loyal, and that tells me something. The crew's loyal and did his bidding at all costs, and that tells me something. A good man but a hard one, who got harder and harder as he got sicker and sicker. That be about right?"

Gonzales stared quietly, melancholy piercing his worn, weathered face.

"Will you take your chances with me, or with the army?"

"With you, Dr. Toole. The more I see of you, the taller you stand with me."

Chapter 9

Together they rode eastward, down the broad Yellowstone valley, alongside the silver rails of the Northern Pacific. The dirt road paralleled the track and never ran far from a cold aquamarine river fed by mountain melt. This time of year the ruts jarred the hoof, but with rain the trail could turn into yellow gumbo that would mire wagons and wear out a horse in a few miles. Lush grass bloomed in the bottoms east of town, and the valuable land had been butchered into pastures and hay meadows by local people. Santiago knew he'd find the great herd up on the dry prairie, away from the claimed bottoms and far from Miles City.

Covertly he glanced at the segundo riding easily on his scrawny cowpony, his dark weathered face expressionless, his bright blue eyes observant, catching the explosion of ducks from a marsh, the tan blur of a coyote, and the circling of an eagle far above. Gonzales, he knew, was a torn man. He had spent a lifetime working faithfully for the Braggs. But now he faced the discovery of crime by the very people he'd given his life to.

"You speak English as well as Spanish, Mr. Gonzales."

The segundo spurred his pony up beside Santiago's taller thoroughbred. "Better, actually. My mother was Alice Parkinson, originally from Virginia until they moved to Corpus Christi. My father, Estaban Gonzales y Ortega, had a large shipping business there. Port, you know. On the Nueces. English, not Spanish, was my childhood language."

"How'd you begin with the Braggs?"

Gonzales glanced at him sharply then smiled faintly. "It wasn't in my blood to spend my days in a musty office in a steamy east-Texas port. I took off as a young man, drifted west, found work with a fierce Anglo named Bragg who had burned a brand onto every slick cimarron he could lasso. I had a way with cattle and men, both Anglo and Mexican. So I stayed and he rewarded me well. Some of this herd are my own beeves."

"You still have a way with men, Mr. Gonzales."

"I'm not sure of that. I'd better warn you, Sheriff, this crew will probably face you down."

"Will they obey you?"

"Some will. Some definitely will not if obeying means cooperating with a Montana sheriff. Others will wait to hear what Apollo says."

"They'd obey a twelve-year-old boy?"

"He's a Bragg, Sheriff. It's his brand."

"What do you think will happen?"

"They'll say you've got Miss Athena in jail."

"I see."

"No, you don't see. They talk of freeing her, tearing up Miles, hoorawing the town, and taking off. You're more doctor than sheriff, and they're ready to prove it to you."

"They might be surprised," said Santiago softly. This was a thing he'd encountered in hard men over and over.

"How'd you ever get to be a sheriff anyway?"

"Oh, lots of things. When I first came to Miles there were maybe three hundred people, mostly ruffians. I did a little business pulling lead out of them, but the practice didn't amount to much. About two hundred cash dollars a year plus a few chickens, a horse or two, some vegetables, and half-a-dozen saddles and bridles. I had time, lots of it. They made an offer, temporary of course, until they could get a real lawman, tough as nails and all that. I ended up liking it, and they discovered I'd learned a few dainty things in my life, such as shooting and brawling."

"You have a little lilt, an accent."

"Ireland, lad. Where I learned to brawl with the best."

"Then why — "

"A thing called primogeniture, Mr. Gonzales. Lands and titles go to the oldest son. Younger sons are gotten rid of so they don't linger close to home and cause trouble. The army absorbs most of them. Others get remittances to stay away. My father had other notions and packed me off to Edinburgh to master medicine at the university."

"But why here, Mr. Toole?"

Santiago drew into himself, feeling the ancient pain. "Because — it's not even a wee bit like home."

The bite of his voice shut off further inquiry. They'd exchanged pasts, and that was that.

At a point Santiago estimated to be six miles downriver from Miles, the segundo abandoned the Keogh-Bismarck road and steered them up a long coulee piercing southward, flanked by slopes of buffalo grass. Santiago followed, lost in his reveries. He really didn't know how to handle this one. Apollo tugged at him. Medicine and law tore at him.

He'd learned long ago that the healing arts really dealt with soul as well as body, and that if he ignored souls, he wouldn't heal much. The only diseased thing about

Apollo Bragg was his soul, and Santiago hoped to heal it. Hermes Bragg had lacerated his own son and wrecked his own daughter. Maybe, Santiago thought, a sheriff should mind his own business, let the Braggs all suffer whatever was due them under the law, and let it go at that. But the image of the torn boy lingered in his mind; a boy wanting to break free from iron bonds not just to be himself, but to do what seemed right to him.

So far, at least, Santiago had little hard evidence of a crime. He'd seen a few recently branded beeves in a large herd. That proved nothing. There'd been a fight of some sort, allegedly with Sioux, but he had no proof of it, no word from Fort Robinson or the Sioux agent at Pine Ridge. Whatever happened it'd been enough to turn the whole Bragg crew into a closemouthed outfit that wouldn't even whoop it up in a town that catered to whooping drovers.

When they topped the head of the coulee, they rode out upon high prairie with mile-long grassy slopes and sharp escarpments covered with jackpine. The whole country seemed alive with toy cattle, dots on a vast straw canvas. A lot of beef. One family's entire fortune. One segundo's entire fortune, too. And wages for a dozen-and-a-half men.

All of it stalled here because of Santiago. He knew that when they arrived at the cow camp he'd find few friends and even fewer allies. It would be up to Gonzales, he thought. And Apollo.

They rode through knots of grazing beeves and other animals settled comfortably on clay ground working their cud. Within ten minutes Santiago spotted seven HB brands with a fresh *H*. He detoured for a closer look, while Gonzales followed dourly.

"Mr. Gonzales," he said. "You could save me a tally and your crew a lot of work if you'd give me a number and an explanation."

"I work for the Braggs."

"You're a loyal man, and I admire that."

"I'll let the Braggs do their own explaining."

The exchange hung between them as they jogged the last half mile to camp. The outfit had chosen well, in the lee of a bluff with a spring at its base that ultimately fed a pencil-thin creek down the coulee to the Yellowstone.

Ten men were in camp, not counting Apollo, and none of them friendly, Santiago thought. The rest would be out circling the great herd.

At the chuck wagon a big dark cook with giant shoulders stared amiably. Young Apollo looked frightened. Several of the cowboys wore battered side arms, but only one of them worried Santiago. Corkscrew. The slat-ribbed youth with raptor eyes measured graves as Santiago and Gonzales dismounted and stomped life back into legs that had been long in the saddle. Something yellow kindled in Corkscrew's eyes, and his arms twitched with pleasure. He would savor the moment, delay, taunt first. Santiago sighed, as much from the hot threat of doom he saw flaring in Corkscrew's eyes as from the knowledge that he might have to put a bullet into the cowboy. It ran against his whole medical instinct. And yet, he occasionally sliced people open with a scalpel and laid waste to their insides ultimately to heal them. A bullet was only faster surgery.

Jefferson Gonzales offered no introductions, and the crew offered no greetings. Santiago thought to leave them alone with their thoughts for a while. He walked quietly over to Apollo, who watched him somberly from the grass near his wagon. A freshly killed brown prairie rattler with the rattles cut off dangled from the raised tongue.

"Let's go for a walk, son."

"I'll stay here with my crew."

"I thought I'd tell you how your father's doing, and all about Miss Athena, and maybe

139

offer a little advice. You're the man in charge here. Whatever you decide, your crew will do. Right?"

The boy nodded.

"Well, then?"

"I'll make my own decisions."

"I hope you do. Make your decisions and live with them and take the consequences."

The boy peered up uncertainly and then rose. Every man in camp had heard the exchange and stared grimly. Gonzales watched, his wrinkled face expressionless. Santiago suddenly realized that Gonzales wasn't really old; he'd simply weathered and blistered and dried into a mass of wrinkles. Gonzales would keep the peace. Even now those piercing azure eyes stared down the few itchy hands.

"You're walking to get out of their earshot. So you can push on me when I'm alone. And if I cave in, they'll say I'm not a Bragg. And if that happens, I might as well turn it over to Athena and go back home."

"Your pa's some better. Fever's down. Under a hundred."

"So?"

The boy looked miserable. Plainly something in him hungered for his father to live, and something in him dreaded it.

Santiago shrugged. "He's not yelling the

way he did. He looks at me calmly, just like he used to look at you and your sister and his crew. That's good, don't you think?"

"I don't know."

"It's good, lad. But I don't want to hold out false hopes. His lungs — there's not much left. Congested, blasted, cavernous where tissue's been destroyed by the bacilli — "

"What's that?"

The boy knew nothing about germs. "Tiny organisms, much too small for the naked eye to see, that cause many of our diseases. We're just beginning to learn about them."

"You funning me?"

"Those organisms are destroying your father. And that's why I wanted you to wash when you got close to him."

"Why are you here? I want a direct answer."

"For a brand inspection. I want your cooperation."

"You've got my sister in jail."

"For shooting at me. You saw it."

"She raised the shotgun and shot over your head."

"Shot spreads, lad. She barely missed my head. That's called attempted murder."

"She just wanted to scare you."

"That's called a variety of other things, all of which are against the law."

"When you've got Athena in jail you won't

get any help from me. You can't do that to a Bragg."

"Are you exempt from the law of the land?"

"Braggs make our own laws. That's what Father says. Every one who ever amounted to anything does. He says public laws are made by preachers and lawyers and crooks trying to stomp the rest of us or tell everyone what to do."

"What does Apollo say? Not Hermes, but Apollo?"

The boy slid into silence.

"You're in charge here. You can think and act for yourself, Apollo."

"I'm going back," Apollo said, whirling away. He walked fiercely toward the cow camp, while Santiago paced easily behind.

He knew he faced trouble as soon as he arrived in camp. The drovers all wore side arms now and had spread themselves into a large semicircle. Santiago's big bay had been led somewhere out of sight. Only the cook continued his work at the fire. Gonzales stared stonefaced at his own men. At the center of the semicircle stood the one called Corkscrew, strange fires flaring in his colorless eyes.

Something tightened in Santiago's chest, and he felt raw fear. These men stood well

142

apart, spaced for battle, and they looked tough and ready for anything. He'd rarely encountered a deck as stacked as this one, and he felt his heart begin its ascent and his blood begin to pound in his temples.

"We'll do a brand inspection now," the sheriff said. "I want you to gather cattle in bunches and run them past me slowly. I'll want your papers. Mr. Gonzales, if you will direct your men to begin — "

"Cut the crap, Sheriff," said Corkscrew. "Or is it Doc? Or neither?"

"I don't believe I know your name, lad."

The one called Corkscrew laughed. "I'm what my friends call me. Ones who want my born name aren't friends."

"Mr. Gonzales?"

The segundo stared back woodenly.

"Apollo?"

The boy toed the earth a few yards to Santiago's left. "I think we'd better do it," he said.

"Braggs don't talk like that," said Corkscrew. "Toole, if you want to get out of here alive, you just send your jail keys back with Apollo there. When he brings Athena with him, I'll give you your chance. You'll fight your way out."

Prisoner. He turned to Apollo. "Is that your wish, young man?"

143

Apollo nodded, scared and desolate.

"Are you a part of this, Mr. Gonzales?"

The segundo didn't respond. Santiago sensed that he'd been overridden and threatened with death. He thought to argue, threaten them with the law, and then thought better of it. They knew perfectly well what they were doing and knew just as well how thin the law could be here in Montana Territory. He thought to ask them if they meant to kill a doctor, indeed the doctor who was treating their boss and their colleagues. But he decided against that, too. This had gone beyond talk.

"Unbuckle that holster belt, Toole. Or do ya want to try me?" Blood lust lay upon Corkscrew's intent face.

"No, I don't suppose that's necessary," Santiago said quietly.

He hated what he had to do. Whenever doctor and sheriff clashed in him, he hated it, hated the hard decisions. Sheriff won this time. Almost always, in hard corners, sheriff won over doctor.

He did not unbuckle his belt. Instead he walked quietly toward Apollo while armed men watched suspiciously. When the drovers finally understood, it was too late. Santiago simply walked behind the boy and clasped the young man to him, at the same time drawing his sleek Remington.

Corkscrew dug for his gun and stopped suddenly. Jefferson Gonzales had acted faster than the drovers and pointed his battered six-gun at Corkscrew.

"Anyone shoots at Apollo Bragg or the Doc, he's dead before he tries," Gonzales said softly. The segundo backed up to where he could survey the whole semicircle of drovers, who stood, carefully frozen. Some drovers looked relieved.

Santiago Toole sighed. An ally. "Much obliged, Mr. Gonzales. Apologies to you, Apollo. You'll be coming with me. Mr. Gonzales, have them produce my horse."

Gonzales nodded to one of the Mexicans, and the wiry man trotted swiftly toward a brush-choked draw.

Santiago felt the boy tremble in his grip. "We'll talk about it later, lad. I'm taking you to see your pa and your sister now."

"Let me go!"

Santiago didn't. He waited for the vaquero to bring the big bay thoroughbred and motioned the man to go wide around the semicircle of armed drovers. He didn't want anything between him and the ones he watched.

"Mr. Gonzales, I'll remember this. Now if you'll watch these gents, I'll be leaving with Apollo. I think I'm going to arrange a little family conference. I'd take it kindly if you'd explain to these men that their employer is less fevered and resting quietly. I think perhaps a family picnic among the Braggs might — "

"Coward. Hiding behind a boy," taunted Corkscrew.

"Feeling cheated are you?"

"You're not worth fighting, Sheriff."

"You're alive," replied Santiago.

He backed himself and the boy to the horse, swung aboard, and offered a free stirrup to Apollo. The lad swung on behind. He steered toward the great coulee, his back prickling even though the boy sat behind him.

The tension seeped away from him as they jolted downslope toward the Yellowstone. The boy remained silent, not invading Santiago's own bitter mood.

"Are you arresting me?" he asked at last.

Santiago thought he could, actually. He had plenty to throw at the boy if he chose to. Throw it and be done with the damned Braggs and their overbearing ways. Slap this punk into jail for a few weeks. Run them up before Pericles Shaw and let the old goat terrorize them.

He didn't answer.

146

"I guess you are," Apollo concluded.

Santiago didn't feel like talking and rode quietly back to Miles City. He had two patients to visit, both in town fortunately. He had evening rounds. He had to attend to two gunshot Mexicans in the cell as well as Hermes Bragg. He would have to check with Chang Loon and make sure about jail food. And he had to figure out what to do next with this Bragg outfit. He had to crack their silence — either that or find out what happened from other sources. He'd come to respect their silence. Not even Gonzales, a good man, felt ready to talk. He didn't even know what to do with the boy riding behind him up the river valley, along rails turned pewter in the long afternoon light. He didn't know whether the afternoon resulted in defeat or victory. He didn't get the chance to examine brands. He did face down ten armed men ready to kill him.

And all that was nothing compared to Corkscrew's taunts and insults. In all his years of sheriffing, he'd managed to avoid the nonsense of shoot-outs. He didn't give a hoot about his reputation as a lawman and didn't suppose, as some men did, that he had to have a reputation for toughness to curb the ruffians who rode into Miles. He'd always gotten the job done, and that's what counted. But this time the thing came to him, seeking him out, and not letting him go.

Chapter 10

The boy watched while Santiago curried the powerful bay and forked some prairie hay into its manger. Then the doctor watered and hayed his big dray, Mick, and turned to the white-frame cottage in the chill twilight. Summer evanesced daily now, and the cool arrived sooner each evening. A deep, troubled silence weighted the boy as he followed Santiago. They paused in the summer kitchen where Hermes Bragg lay curled, sleeping on his cot. His breathing was regular but thunderous with the rush of air around the tubercules that hung like stalactites in the caverns in his lungs. Santiago doubted the man's rally would last long.

They found Mimi in the kitchen, quietly setting another place for the young visitor. She read Santiago's face as well as the boy's. She could do that, he thought. Without words she knew much of what happened to her husband.

"Wash, lad. There's a pitcher and bowl in there."

The boy slid to an alcove and scrubbed his hands with a ball of soap and returned looking puzzled.

"Are you putting me in jail?"

"What do you think I should do, Apollo?"

The boy turned stony.

"People who break laws go to jail. People who steal what belongs to others or hurt others go to jail. Some people end up in jail for just going along with a crime and not trying to stop it."

The boy stared fearfully at him.

"No, lad, I'm not putting you in jail. Not to lock up, anyway. We'll go make a bed for you because I haven't any other place to put you, but I won't lock you up. You'll be able to walk out."

"Next to Athena?"

"Next to Miss Athena. I don't like to see her in there either, but — well, me lad, I think she committed some crimes, and she thinks she doesn't have to account for them because she's a Bragg, and so we'll have a trial."

Anger flared in the boy's face and then faded. "You've got no right — " he began, but his voice died.

"Your father's a bit better, lad. You saw that. Do you think he might be a different man if he gets well?"

"He'll always be the same."

Mimi summoned them, and they settled quietly at the battered white table. The fare would be simple tonight: boiled potatoes,

150

cabbage, and slabs of beef. She'd poured a glass of thick milk for Apollo.

The boy plunged a fork into a potato, but Santiago stayed him.

"Wait, lad. Grace. Bless us O Lord, and these thy gifts . . ."

He and Mimi blessed themselves while the boy stared. "The Mexicans do that," he said. "Can I eat now?"

Mimi nodded and smiled. "Santo, Mrs. Gatz wants you to go to her. She has catarrh. And that gambler, Jubal Peach, wants more Vapo-Cresolene and a bottle of Thedford's Velio Syrup. And Chang Loon wishes to be paid. And the county says to stop using the jail as a hospital again or they'll take it from your pay."

"Out of seventy-five dollars a month," Santiago retorted sourly. "When they build me a hospital I'll stop using the jail."

Between stabs at beef and cabbage, he told her of the afternoon's events.

"Oh, Santo. I never know when you go away if you'll come home." She turned to Apollo. "It's you Braggs. Your father out there! And if Santo got shot, would you care? Would you?"

Her ferocity cowed the boy, and he turned his gaze to his plate.

Santiago spoke. "That Corkscrew. He looks

familiar. I think I'll go through the dodgers. Most dodgers aren't worth the paper they're printed on, but some new ones, with the photographic image on them . . . Lad, what's Corkscrew's name?"

"I never heard any."

Santiago wolfed his meal, wanting to tackle a dozen chores before night. "Hurry, lad," he muttered. "We'll go look in on Montoya. And your sister."

"Santo, I'm coming with you. I've been thinking all day. I'm going to talk to her. I think I can help."

"Mimi, that girl's going to blow like a keg of giant powder when I walk in there. That tongue of hers is a rasp that'll scrape flesh off anyone within fifty yards."

"I'm going, Santo. She has no mother and a mad father."

Apollo glared at her and then subsided into his food again.

"I'm going to go hug her."

"Mimi — you don't know what kind of people these Braggs are," he said it sharply and let it land on the boy.

"Just the same, Santo, she's a fourteen-year-old girl."

That settled it. She did exactly as she chose. "All right, come then. Stuff your ears with cotton first."

"She doesn't need your help," said Apollo.

"Of course not," said Mimi. "You don't need my help either. I'm not offering help. I'm going there to make friends."

"She doesn't care for breeds."

Mimi paused. "Many of my mother's people, the Assiniboin, don't care for whites who come to cheat them, take their land, kill the buffalo, and . . . make the young men drunk. I tell them some whites are good, some evil, some good but driven along by different ways and hopes and beliefs that hurt others. Where you Braggs plan to settle is a country my people once hunted — along with the Piegans. I see both sides. My father was French and I was schooled in St. Louis by the sisters for many years. I'll tell Athena these things, and we'll see, Apollo."

While Mimi scraped dishes and left them to soak in a pan of hot water drawn from the woodstove reservoir, Santiago organized the extracts and powders in his Gladstone, remembering a blue bottle and a tin for Peach, who ran most of the faro and poker tables in Miles City and probably was a laudanum addict of sorts.

Santiago kept wondering why he treated Apollo so carefully. Any other sheriff would have dumped the lad in the lockup and let him stew there until he talked. And the girl, too, all chivalry aside, given a stormy creature like that. Let 'em taste life behind bars and accept the consequences. Let 'em live under the brutal thumb of a wild father, unable to bend. Let 'em try their Bragging in Montana. That was the sheriff in him. The doctor in him wasn't so sure.

He found Mimi with a black shawl over her shoulders, waiting for him at the picket fence gate. He glanced covertly at his wife, loving her, loving the way the shawl pinned her straight jet hair to her back. She looked strong and Indian in the dusk.

At the jail office he lit a lamp and headed into the cellroom. The smell of Chang Loon's rice and beef lingered. And something else. How did he usually sense such things?

He saw motion at the rear cell as Athena Bragg unfolded from her plank bench and gripped the bars.

"I despise that slop," she said. "I threw it in his face. I want meat. I want this stinking pail cleaned. When I get out of here I'm going to — "

"Careful what you threaten," muttered Santiago, threading into the cell that held his two patients. Mimi and Apollo followed silently, casting long wobbling shadows in the amber light of the lantern.

From one bench the one named José stared

up at him somberly, an empty tan bowl beside him. The pail stank in this cell, unattended because Santiago had no one to attend to it. The county wouldn't let him hire a full-time deputy or even a turnkey.

The other one, Alonzo Montoya, lay too quietly. Santiago slid down beside him and clasped his cold hand. The doctor pulled out his stethoscope and listened to silence. He sighed. The man had died alone in a cell. Faster than he'd expected. He had intended to be here, help the man through his last passage, allay terror and loneliness. But he'd been pulled away — sheriff duties — and the illness had descended faster than he'd expected. He stared at the body, its soul and awareness elsewhere now. Quietly he folded Montoya's hands across the man's chest and bowed his head. What could a doctor do but pray for the soul of those he failed to save? He felt guilty because his duties had pulled him away. Sometimes law and medicine tore at each other, and he wondered why he didn't settle on one or the other.

"Gone," he said. "Another gone."

The other Mexican stared fearfully and blessed himself. Santiago sat down on the other bench and held the man's warm hand in his own a minute. The living grieved the

155

dead. José gripped the doctor's hand and wept, muttering things Santiago didn't understand.

"Get him out of here," wailed Athena. "I can't stand it."

Santiago contained his retort and began examining José quietly. The man had come along well. The dim lantern light revealed no suppuration in the mouth, no pus or drainage from the cheek.

"Apollo, tell this one he's fine. He doesn't need to stay here. He can go to the cow camp. I'll leave some gargle and some carbolic. He's to keep everything clean and wipe the wound with carbolic frequently. If he hasn't a horse, he's welcome to stay here."

Apollo softly translated while José listened with wet eyes and glistening dark cheeks. He sat up, stared at the dead man on the other bench, and buried his head in his hands. Mimi settled beside him, sliding an arm over the man's thick shoulders.

The cell stank of urine, sweat, pus, and death.

Santiago dropped his stethoscope into his bag, defeated. Now it'd be Sylvane Tobias's turn. He stood wearily, the trials of the day heavy on him — a scrape with death in the sunny afternoon and the loss of a patient now — and wondered if he ought to abandon the sheriffing. He picked the kerosene lamp off the rock floor and made his way back to the rear cell.

"That's two," he said to the girl. "I suppose somewhere back there in Texas or Mexico a mother or father or sister or wife or children will weep, and miss him."

"It's not my fault."

"I thought you might feel some responsibility, lass. Your father employed them. You must have known them well after several months on the trail."

"I never associate with wage men."

"How about it, Miss Bragg? Do you grieve?"

"I want that pail cleaned. I want water. I want to wash. I want a meal instead of slop. I want clean clothes. I want a blanket and a pillow. I hate being in the same place with that dead man. I want him out. Give me a direct answer: are you going to get him out and help me?"

Apollo joined her. "I don't want to stay here tonight."

"Because a man died here?"

"Because of ghosts. He might haunt me and Athena."

"Maybe you should be haunted."

The boy's eyes filled with tears, and Santiago wished he hadn't said it. The lad wasn't at fault. Santiago wasn't even certain Hermes

Bragg was at fault or any crime had been committed.

"Lad, lad, I have a mean tongue, and I'm sorry. We'll make a place for you in our cottage, my wife and I."

"I'll tell Pa you cried," Athena taunted. "No ghost can scare me."

Santiago found the cell key and swung open the barred door. "There's a closet with a basin and pitcher just off my office, young lady." The girl peered at him, startled, and headed toward the front of the cellroom. "Mimi, I've some cleaning to attend to here. Perhaps you could look after these young people — "

Mimi found the hand of the weeping boy and escorted him forward while Toole plucked up the stinking tin bucket and the other foul bucket from José's cell and toted them out. Jailkeeping wasn't exactly his line of work, but things needed doing, and he did them. The wounded Mexican drover watched him impassively.

Two dead, one injured, and two children half-brutalized by a man who'd been driven by demons. Two friendless children. Two motherless children. Two children with millstones around them who couldn't be children, couldn't grow up and do what boys and girls do, couldn't even become a man or a

158

woman because they were being turned into slaves of property and the victims of one man's monstrous conceit. Santiago slipped out into the sharp night, dumped the pails, limed the privy, rinsed the foul containers with water from the hand pump, and returned them to the cells. The stench of the cellroom smacked him as he entered it. The whole cellroom needed a brooming, so he did that while he waited for Athena Bragg.

No turnkey. No deputy except for emergencies. So far he'd managed a small-town practice that didn't keep him very busy and the sheriff's office, which didn't either. Territorial statute required counties to employ a full-time sheriff, but the county commissioners had winked at it. They had come to him when the county was barely organized and Miles City had scarcely three hundred denizens, mostly ruffians and buffalo-hide hunters. Take it part time, they'd said. Temporary, of course. Santiago smiled. The good burghers of Milestown, as they called it then, discovered Sheriff Toole had spent a youth brawling in Ireland, was a master of arms, and was able to hold his own with brutes twice his weight.

Athena Bragg took her own sweet time but eventually emerged looking scrubbed. She'd given herself a spit bath, but her clothes remained grimy.

"All right, lass. Back we go."

"I'm hungry."

"That's your problem. You were served wholesome food by Chang Loon."

"Slop!"

Santiago caught her arm and steered her into the black bowel of the cellroom.

"I don't want to go in there!"

"I'm on my way right now to Sylvane Tobias, who takes care of the dead here. He's a cabinetmaker, actually. He'll pick up the remains in an hour."

"Santo," said Mimi, "let her sit here in the office with us. I'll watch over her. We'll talk."

"I can't do that, Mimi," he said wearily. "I'm not even supposed to leave this building unattended when there are prisoners in it. But they won't give me a deputy."

For once she didn't resist. He caught the bail of a hurricane lamp and took the fuming girl back to her cell.

"It stinks," she said.

He swung the door shut on her and locked it.

"They'll get me out. They'll come and break me out."

"Thanks for the warning."

That might happen, he thought. The whole

160

wild bunch of Texans could whoop into sleepy Miles City and take over the building with no resistance, busting the girl out. Maybe hurting whoever was here . . . like Mimi.

"I'll be back directly," he said.

José still lay on his pallet, keeping vigil next to the body of Montoya, watching Santiago pass by with dull eyes. A weariness ran through the sheriff, and he wondered if he was ill. In his office he found Mimi and the boy, waiting silently.

"Apollo? Come along with me, lad. We'll go for a little walk." Toole pulled on his black frock coat against the chill.

The boy rose listlessly, dry-eyed. Mimi stood, too.

"Santo? I want to go make friends with that girl."

"She'll bite your head off, Mimi."

"I don't care. I'm going back in. I'll sit in the next cell and talk."

Some dread filled Santiago. "Mimi — if anyone comes to break that girl out — if Bragg cowboys and toughs come in . . ."

"Go get Sylvane Tobias."

He slid out the office door and stood on the stoop, listening to the night. He heard peace. He hiked down to Park Street. Apollo joined him silently, and they walked eastward on Main Street and then north around a building to an apartment at the rear.

Sylvane Tobias answered his knock, a cut-glass stein of pilsner in his hand and slippers on his blue-veined feet. "I know, I know," he said. "You got another. That Mexican. I went in there this afternoon and smelled the mortifying. I should have dug that Mexican hole a little wider and waited. Are they going to pay or the county?"

"I don't rightly know, Sylvane."

"If you don't know, I'll just wrap him in a sheet and forget the box and dump him in. The less Mex, the better. I hear the Sioux put some lead pills into 'em. Did the world a favor, them Injuns. Maybe all them colored will kill each other off."

"You'll pay the dead your respects, Tobias," snapped Santiago.

"I don't rightly see why. Who's this rascal?"

"He's Apollo Bragg."

Tobias peered closer at the boy, not seeing much in the dim light. "Ah, the boy. Sister's in the hoosegow, and the old man's dying of consumption on your porch. Three shot Mex in your pokey. Some outfit. What's the boy done beside get Mexicans shot up?"

Apollo straightened himself up. "I haven't done anything. And my pa and me, we like

162

Mexicans. And Texans, too."

Santiago laughed.

"And I'll pay for a good burying. I'll get it from our trail boss. And it's going to be right or I'll not pay."

Tobias muttered. "One of them that don't see the natural distinctions laid down by nature red in tooth and claw. You got to be a Mason to understand. All right, all right, Toole. Let me pull some boots over my bunions and harness old Hell — "

"Not Hell. Harness Heaven, Sylvane."

"I'll harness what's fitting, Sheriff. I suppose you want a hole dug in the middle of the night, too."

"Do it tomorrow."

"Now ain't you techy. You look tired, Toole."

"Long day and I still have night rounds and some calls to make."

They left Tobias to his mutterings and walked slowly back to the jail through a dark and quiet evening.

"I don't want to sleep there. Not with that haunt," the boy said. "He'll come after me and Athena in the night. I know it."

"All right, lad. How about my barn? Prairie hay in the loft and a blanket."

"I'd like that," he said. "Dr. Toole? It aint the Mexicans' fault. My pa made them

163

do it. He made all of us do it, even when Jefferson Gonzales got mad and told them not to. Pa sat up in the wagon with two scatterguns and told them they had to or ride out without wages."

Chapter 11

Santiago found Hermes Bragg resting quietly the next morning, a ray of sun catching the man's sunken face and giving false color to his wasted flesh. Heart arrhythmic. Lungs thunderous. Yellow sputum caked about the man's dry lips. Lymph glands, what was left of them, as lumpy as gravel. A powerful body collapsed by the relentless work of the bacilli Koch had discovered over the past year.

"What's my boy doing here?" Bragg asked with that hollow rasp of his ulcerated larynx.

Santiago ignored the question. "Montoya's dead. That wound through his thigh mortified. He was brought to me too late for amputation. It was complicated by pneumonia. That's two men gone, Bragg. Was it worth it?"

Bragg stared at some space of his own making below the whitewashed planks over the summer kitchen. The man's eyes had softened today and didn't have the febrile brightness in them that spoke of demons to a careful observer. "Montoya was a good man," he said. "So was Iturbide."

"I thought you preferred to shoot horses

with broken legs," Santiago retorted.

"Wage men. You can't let yourself worry about wage men. Now give me a direct answer, Toole. Why's my boy here?" The man's opaque dark eyes focused on Santiago as if he were a manservant.

"Ask him," Toole replied. "He's free to go where he chooses."

"You're not holding him?"

"That's correct. I'm holding your daughter, though."

"She's tougher than you'll ever be, Toole. You'll end up sorry you done it. She'll get you good. Don't get mad, get even. I raised her that way."

Santiago dropped his stethoscope into his Gladstone and dug around for the white vitriol. "How did you raise them, Bragg? I'm curious. Where was Mrs. Bragg? What was her name?"

Bragg paused, weighing the question. "Her name doesn't matter. I call her the children's mother. I won't give her a name."

"Divorced?"

"No. I sent her away. She's in San Antonio."

"What was her crime?"

"Raising my children weak, Toole. Raising them soft. Them that was left. First two died of diptheria, the next of the typhoid."

"Holy Mary. Soft, Bragg?"

166

"Hard country takes hard people. Comanche bullets and arrows ain't love letters. They don't listen to please and thank you and grace before chow. She never got that through her head, so I did what I had to. Sent her packing."

"That was her crime, Bragg? Gentling her little ones?"

"Soft ones die in that land, Toole."

"And you sent her away for that?"

"I did. I told her never to enter my door again. I told her I wouldn't divorce her because she didn't deserve a man." Bragg's eyes gleamed with strange, hot rectitude.

"How'd she take that?"

"She wept, all soft, more than a man should take, and I had to escort her to her buggy. Toole, in that hard country, what she done was worse than if she'd took up with someone."

Loathing flooded through Santiago, but he kept it in check. He'd learned that the American frontier sometimes twisted and darkened mortals in ways beyond anything he'd imagined possible in Ireland.

"Pretty rough on the babies. I assume they were small?"

"Oh, they bawled some, like a weaned calf. But I whaled them for bawling and that stopped it."

"Now they never cry."

"Never. I'd take a bullwhip to them if they did."

"Now they'll carry on exactly as you wish, your stamp and brand on them, Bragg. Tough as you and stamped in your image."

Bragg paused again, letting silence tick out his scorn. "Tougher, Toole. Tougher, even if you don't like it. This is wilderness. Frontier ain't even come here. That Judith country, that's where Blackfeet run. I fitted my boy and girl to whup them good. Whether I'm around or not."

The man's voice had gone thick. He coughed convulsively, already near the end of his strength. The muslin rag he coughed into showed ruby specks. Maybe the news about Montoya would end his rally. But Toole doubted it. Odd thing: the sheriff part of him wanted to hammer at Bragg, get a confession out of him. The doctor part knew it'd kill the man fast and wanted to nurture Bragg along, give him the weeks or months that his powerful body might yet snatch of life.

"You're holding on, Bragg. But this summer kitchen's going to be too cold soon, and I'll have to move you. If you stay flat on your back, eat well, maybe you'll buy some time. If you want it. You might not.

You'll be a prisoner of a cot every hour you live."

Bragg glared at the doctor from bitter eyes and then settled back. "Where's my herd?"

"Still east of town on good bedground."

"What's happening to Athena?"

"Trial in a week. Before the justice, Pericles Shaw. For shooting at me, resisting arrest, preventing me from examining brands. Especially the ones with new road brands on the near shoulder."

"Saw those, did you? Well, she did right. Wish she'd blasted you to hell. You go nosing around Bragg private business, you end up paying good for it. Anyone knows that where I come from. You just lack the lesson yet, Sheriff."

"You want to talk about those new brands?"

"Toole, there's a rule in my country. You take every cow you can because if you don't the next man will. I take whatever cows I get ahold of. Lost half my herds to outfits that took every animal of mine they could drop a loop on and brand. It all adds up, and the stronger the man, the better the chance to survive it."

"That's a hard way, Bragg."

"Only way. Do it or get robbed out, beaten down, cheated by all them neighbors that smiled howdy, stole blind by every cowboy who could register his mark and beat you out to the paired-up stock when new grass came. Beat them down and someday you can see fat stock grazing your hills and the ones who used you six hard feet under."

"You don't trust your men."

"Why should I? I've hung three, caught red-handed. Whipped others and sent them off."

"That's a puzzle, Bragg. They're all loyal. They'd do anything for you, even put your mark on cattle that belong to someone else. Yet you treat them like galley slaves, tell your children to shoot any horse with a broken leg, so to speak — and there they are, loyal. Gonzales, now — a lifetime of devotion to you. Proud to work for the Braggs. Protective of Miss Athena and Apollo when the young folks need protecting. Very strange, Bragg."

Hermes Bragg grinned lopsidedly, sputum cracking at the corners of his lips, fires flaring in his eyes.

"Doesn't matter what you think, Sheriff. Those rannies get out of line or cheat on me, and I'd blow their heads off."

"I think there's more to it, Hermes Bragg. I think maybe you talk one way and do things another way. You're all wind."

170

"If I had the strength, Toole, I'd be out of bed and teaching you a lesson."

"As I say, Bragg, you're a blowhard. Some call it a bark worse than the bite. All brag, Bragg. Enough bragging and threatening to scare your children witless, wouldn't you say?"

"They don't scare."

Santiago sighed, wondering how far to take this and what the man's body would endure. "You know, Mr. Bragg, your girl could get out fast enough by pleading guilty and paying a fine."

"No Bragg pleads guilty to anything." He coughed violently again. "Nothing left in my bellows to cough up anymore," he muttered. "That girl pleads guilty to anything, I'd have Gonzales whup her good. They've got responsibilities. Two thousand head and a payroll is a responsibility."

Santiago stood. He'd exposed himself far too long to the deadly cough.

"You ever thought of letting your children make their own lives, do what they want to?"

Hermes Bragg hooted and then collapsed into spasms of coughing.

"All right, Mr. Bragg. Get your rest now. But before you sleep, let me tell you what I'm going to do. Sheriff Toole's going to

keep on looking into a possible crime —
stolen cattle. Possible murder. Maybe take
a posse to look at the herd if I keep running
into trouble from your men. Sheriff Toole's
going to find out what happened. Dr. Toole's
going to keep on treating you. And treating
your children. I'll tell you something, Mr.
Bragg. My wife Mimi and I are going to
start undoing what you've done to your children."

Bragg glared daggers from his pillow. His
eyes looked feverish again, Santiago thought.
But he pushed on relentlessly.

"My wife started with Miss Athena last
night. She just sat in the next cell there,
talking with the girl. Not pushing any way
at all. Telling your daughter about herself,
making friends. Offering the girl love. Giving
her the thing you couldn't offer her or Apollo
or your wife. I don't think you drove your
wife away because she raised your children
soft, but because she offered you love, and
you couldn't take it. You're not hard, Mr.
Bragg; you're afraid of something."

Hermes Bragg blinked in spite of himself.

"Doc Toole's befriending Apollo, making
friends, getting to like that fine lad. Getting
him to think on his own, do what he thinks
is right, no matter what you told him to
do. What he wants from life is his own self,

172

not just being some arm or leg of you. Next thing you know, Bragg, Doc Toole's going to do what your wife tried to do — give them their own lives and some care about others."

But Bragg had closed his eyes and fallen asleep, or was feigning it. Toole wetted a rag with carbolic solution and wiped his face and hands carefully. Then he turned into his kitchen and discovered Apollo there, beside the door, looking troubled and stern.

Santiago found Athena Bragg surprisingly willing to come along to Montoya's burial. He thought she might resist, but the dark cell had grated on her, and she welcomed a chance at sunshine and fresh air.

This burial will be on the county, he thought. He did not send word out to the Bragg cow camp for fear the messenger would be held hostage in exchange for Athena. So only four people walked behind Sylvane Tobias's cart with the yellow pine box rattling and bouncing on its bed as Tobias drove up the steep slope to the field of the dead on the bluff. Toole himself led, dressed in his black frock coat and vest, with a string tie and flat-crowned hat. Beside him the Bragg children traipsed quietly up the slope. And a few steps behind lumbered José, whose shattered mouth had mended enough for him to abandon the jail cot. He'd spend a last night there for want of a horse to carry him out to the cow camp.

The morning lay rawboned and cold with a harsh Montana gale cutting through them all. Sylvane Tobias sat in a greatcoat, hunched over the lines guiding his dray. He'd hooked the gray, Purgatory, to the cart that morning and summoned the sheriff for the brief ceremony. Santiago glanced covertly at the girl, who strode with dour purpose beside him. This trip was, in a sense, for her benefit. They were about to bury a Bragg hand, a good man, dead because of something Athena's father had done. He wanted her to see this, hear it, feel it, and discover somewhere in her small, mean heart that Braggs had toyed with mortal lives, and someone back in Texas would weep for Montoya. He planned to drive the thought home with a short eulogy for the vaquero. Drive it home hard, before an audience of two children, a Mexican who wouldn't understand him, and Sylvane Tobias, who needed a lesson or two himself.

Apollo would benefit from the lesson, too, although Santiago felt that the boy's understanding of the world had already shattered and the youth lay open and tender and eager to live by better codes than he had learned from his father.

Santiago glanced behind him and found José lagging, the climb up the hill too much for a man just out of his sickbed. He paused and offered an arm, but José refused with a brief smile. Grief possessed him, open on his weathered dark face, living in him in a way unknown to Englishmen who buried every emotion they buried with the body. The Irish did it better, he thought, thinking of joyous wakes that had been not only a send-off for the dead, but a celebration of love and friendship. All the wakes he'd attended were a way of grieving that affirmed the soul's triumphant passage and drained away the dark emotions of grief. It was good to grieve, and he wondered why so many northern Europeans dreaded it.

Tobias's wagon hairpinned a turn in the rutted road and headed out across a frost-burned meadow toward a corner of the cemetery. A hole in the yellow clay gaped there beside the new grave of Iturbide, which was marked only with a plank and a painted name. Tobias was against wasting money on Mexicans.

Tobias reined up beside the gloomy hole and slid down. He spread two long, leather straps on the ground and stepped back. Unasked,

Apollo and José stationed themselves at corners of the pine casket while Santiago and Sylvane manned the other corners, and they eased the box to the ground over the straps. Then they carefully lowered the box into the hole and slid the straps away. Santiago removed his black hat, and the vaquero did also. Tobias had worn none. They all stared solemnly at the sheriff, waiting for whatever it was that he would say.

He peered off into the pewter skies, wondering where souls went and what he might say to do honor to a life lost and prick the soul of a girl whose heart lay encased in its own tomb.

"I did not know this man," he began softly. "I was unable to save his life when he was brought to me. I did what I could with all the tools we doctors possess in this year of our Lord 1882. But others knew him. Soon, word of this death will get back to Texas, and there someone will grieve. Perhaps many will grieve. Perhaps this man's mother and father, who nurtured him to manhood. Perhaps his brothers and sisters, who knew and loved him. Perhaps his wife and children, who depended on him for their daily bread and the good things a father brings to his family. Or perhaps he was alone in the world and no one will grieve. Or maybe no one will ever reach his family, and they will never learn of his death here in the northern prairies of Montana."

Good, he thought, both Apollo and Athena were listening intently. He had made his point: that someone had loved this man they buried.

"This man gave his life in the service of his employer, Hermes Bragg," Santiago continued gently. "He gave everything, for life is the ultimate gift. No more will this man greet the sun, hug a wife or children, enjoy a feast, or kneel before his Maker to give thanks and receive gifts. All this he gave up on behalf of his employers. I know that this is really a great loss to each of you, to your father, to you, Apollo, and you, Miss Athena."

The girl looked acutely uncomfortable and darted fierce glances at her brother, who stood somberly, absorbing all as if it were a gentle punishment.

"This is a great loss to José, beside you, who sees a friend being lowered into the earth. A friend he will never see again. So Montoya is grieved among the cowboys and hands who came with him all those months across the continent.

"That is all I have to say. We wish this man's soul Godspeed on its voyage and pray the mercy of God upon him."

The sheriff led them through a short prayer, and it was done.

Wind sliced through their thin clothing. Athena in particular was ill-dressed for the bitter air and still wore the rumpled, soiled clothing she had on when she was arrested. He felt sorry for her and hoped that this, along with other harsh things, would penetrate the whalebone corsets of her soul and free a young woman from her glowering father.

He nodded to Tobias, who seized a shovel and began tossing dirt into the hole. Clods of clay rattled hollowly on the final home of Alonzo Montoya, the sound weak against the shrill whip of the lonely wind. They left Tobias there to complete his task and hurried down toward the comfort of Miles City. Even Athena hastened, although her haste led her back to an eight-foot-square cell with stone walls on two sides and iron bars on the other two. The darkness of the cells erected by the county fathers was a prison in its own right, Santiago thought.

"Miss Athena," he said softly as they walked. "You can always plead guilty, pay a fine, and leave."

"I'm a Bragg," she retorted. "You can't break me."

"I am not trying to. You're not there to be broken but to serve justice."

"You're trying to break me," she retorted but without much force.

He supposed there was a kind of truth in it. In fact, maybe she saw things better than he did. He hoped indeed to break her, though not exactly in the way she supposed. He wanted to free her from the hovering, brutal spirit of her father, which would torture her all her life. In that, he supposed, he was being the doctor rather than the sheriff.

They crossed the plank bridge and went on into town, past the forlorn hulks of whiskey row where saloon signs flapped and clattered in the wind, turning east toward the jail and his office. They walked on in, and only then did he discover he'd made a terrible mistake, the kind of mistake a professional lawman would never make.

Chapter 12

Six drovers lounged in Toole's office, among them the one called Corkscrew. Each held a six-gun, and each six-gun pointed at him, their lethal black bores terrible to behold. Santiago wore no weapon; it wasn't his custom to wear a weapon to a burial. Ahead of him the children had entered, and behind him in the doorway stood José.

"Madre Dios!" the man whispered.

Santiago supposed he might be witnessing his last moments on earth. At a nod from Corkscrew a drover sidled up and parted Santiago's frock coat, finding nothing underneath.

"Got you, Toole," said Corkscrew. "We're taking the girl. We're leaving with the herd. We've waited too long as it is. We're taking the boy, too."

Apollo and Athena both looked frightened, but Athena drew herself up and stared defiantly at Santiago.

"Where's Jefferson Gonzales?" Toole asked.

"Wouldn't you like to know."

"Jailbreak is a criminal offense."

Corkscrew smiled. "We'll be in the Judith country. Come get us, Toole. Send a posse."

Santiago sighed. Judith wasn't in his county. These men knew full well how thin Toole's chance was of ever nabbing them. A deep fear crawled through him, spurred by the unwavering bores of those six guns, any of which could explode at the nervous spasm of a finger.

"I'm unarmed. Put up your weapons, gents. You're likely to hurt Apollo and Miss Athena. Or kill José here."

None of the drovers slid a weapon into its holster, but two lowered the bores toward the plank floor.

"Toole — walk back there." Corkscrew pointed toward the cellroom with his revolver.

"Just a moment," Toole said. "Miss Athena, you're the Bragg in command. If you say so, lass, these men will stop this — "

"Shut up, Toole." Corkscrew lifted the bore of his revolver straight into Santiago's face.

"Do it, Athena!" Apollo blurted.

Athena didn't consider long. "I'm going. I won't go back to that stinking hole for anything on earth."

"I'm not going!" cried Apollo.

"Hell you ain't, sonny," said Corkscrew. "You're a Bragg, and you're going."

"I'm staying. I'm a Bragg and I'm telling you I'm staying."

"Take him," said Athena, grinning.

"We may as well take your pa, too, Miss Athena," said Corkscrew.

Santiago was appalled. "That'll kill him for sure. In bed, he has a chance at life for a while."

"We'll take him."

"At least ask him!" snapped Santiago. "Taking him is murder."

"We'll take him," said Corkscrew.

"And if he says no?"

"We'll take him. We'll get the whole outfit out of your clutches, Toole. I never did cotton to a sheriff being a doctor, too. Just a way of throwing weight around."

"Athena. Are you going to let them kill your father?"

She smiled. "He always said, if a horse breaks a leg, shoot it."

"What if his leg isn't broken, Athena?"

"It's broken."

"What if he says, don't take me? What if he says, no jailbreak? What if he says, go back to cow camp and wait? What if he says — "

"Miss Athena's the boss, ain't it so?" Corkscrew retorted.

She smiled.

Beside Santiago, José muttered and blessed himself.

"We're taking him. And we're taking your squaw wife, Toole. Just for insurance."

Something went cold in Santiago, and he felt dizzy with sudden dread.

Corkscrew grinned. "Didn't like that, did you? I can tell what a man's thinkin'."

No, Santiago thought, he didn't like that. He found himself full of helplessness, surrounded by men bent on dark things, and there was nothing he could do but obey and hope for a break.

"I'd better go with you to my house. If you're taking Hermes Bragg, I'd better send along some powders. Things that'll give him a chance to live."

"Nice try, Toole. But you're going to have a new house for a while until someone saws you out."

"Apollo, have my wife give you laudanum, white vitriol, belladonna, and carbolic. And a ball of soap. Whenever you and Athena are close to your father, or he coughs in your direction, stop and wash yourselves carefully, face and hands."

The boy blinked back tears. Athena noticed and smirked.

"Athena," Santiago said. "Think what you're doing."

"I've already thought. We make our own law, Sheriff. If you doubt it, just try us."

Santiago addressed Corkscrew. "We just buried Alonzo Montoya, who died for the Braggs. If you go ahead with this, more of you will die for the Braggs. The first will be you, Corkscrew. I've seen your face somewhere, on a dodger."

"I'll face you, Toole. Hand him a gun, Shorty."

The ruddy short hand squinted. "I ain't going to do it, Cork. We got business to attend."

Annoyed, Corkscrew nodded. "Someday," he said to Toole.

They prodded him toward a cell, the corner cell Athena had occupied, found the brass key in his pocket, and shoved him in. He watched the barred door creak on its iron hinges and clang shut. Corkscrew snapped the lock, pulled on the door once to make sure, and grinned.

"Taste of your own medicine, Doc."

"I trust you'll leave the key on my desk."

"Why? So you can chase us? No, Toole. It goes with us. After I lock the cellroom door, too. They can saw you out. And by the time you get out, we'll be away from your county."

Santiago held his tongue. He watched them file down the corridor, prodding Apollo with them. The boy glanced back at Santiago, his face fearful. The cellroom door slammed, and he heard the snap of its lock. Darkness permeated the cellroom, the only light coming from the high grilled window. Santiago sat down in the gloom, amid the rising stink of the pail and the rank odor of ancient sweat and spat tobacco. He scarcely thought of himself while visions of Mimi in danger filled his mind.

He looked about him for something to make noise with. If anyone entered his office, he would need to shout and tap on metal to win attention. He found nothing except the tin pail. The boards of the wooden bench bit his tailbone, and the coldness of the cell cut into him. All he could do was wait.

But not for long. A few minutes, in fact. Someone entered his office and then rattled the cell door. Santiago yelled.

Pericles Shaw responded. "Toole? You locked in your pleasure palace?" he barked with that gravelly voice of his.

"Pericles! Get me out!"

"Ah, Toole, what did you do to offend God?" yelled Pericles. The lock snapped, and the justice of the peace lumbered in. "Why look at you, cozied up in there."

Shaw unlocked the cell door and swung it open.

"How'd you know?" asked Santiago.

"I was fixing to send a horsefly perched on my windowsill to perdition when out of my window I observed a strange spectacle, Toole. Our young prisoner escorted toward the rear of the building where horses stood at the hitch rail by gentlemen with artillery in hand peering sharply back toward Main Street. They prodded along a young man I assume — from town gossip — to be young Bragg. And last came the heavy Mexican, quite unarmed, the very one who endured the county pokey for a hospital. They had a plug waiting for him."

"Anyone else, Pericles? Tell me fast."

"No. No one was back holding the horses, Toole. You'll congratulate me for my forbearance. I didn't shoot at that horsefly, but I found it guilty and fined it a dollar. If it cannot pay, it'll face the tumbrils."

"You didn't see the segundo, Gonzales?"

"No, Toole, he wasn't in this little party."

"Pericles — thanks. My wife's in danger. I have to get to my house." Santiago plunged up the aisle, the justice lumbering after him. He buckled his belt and holstered the Remington about his waist, where the holster made a bulge in his frock coat.

"You want help?"

"No, Pericles."

He trotted out, into blinding light although

the day was overcast, and ran up Main Street. Fear knotted within him. He felt his heart answer the pumping of his legs, and he ran all the harder when he got his wind. He swung off Main, toward his cottage — and saw nothing. No horses. He stopped, his lungs pumping, and then edged swiftly around toward his barn where the horses might be. He crept toward the rear of the carriage barn, peered through a knothole, and found his own stalled horses and nothing else.

They'd taken her then! He slammed forward to the summer kitchen and yanked open the door. Hermes Bragg lay in his cot, staring and laughing hoarsely. At the door to the house stood Mimi, a shawl over her shoulders and a derringer in her hand.

"Mimi!" he cried. "Thank God!"

"I was coming, Santo! I was just coming!"

"What happened?"

Bragg laughed coarsely and ended up coughing. "She buffaloed 'em. Some squaw you got, Toole!"

"They rode up, Santo. The cowboys with six-guns in their hands. With Apollo and Athena. And a spare horse. And you weren't with them. So I get my derringer from my reticule, and I set down on the cot beside Mr. Bragg, and I pointed the derringer at his head."

187

Bragg laughed raucously.

"They came in and said they were going to take him and me, too. I said I'd kill him if they made the slightest move."

Santiago listened, astonished at his wife.

"They didn't believe me and started to come, but Hermes Bragg believed me and told them to stop. He told them to go and start the last of the drive and begin the ranch."

"And they obeyed Hermes Bragg," said Santiago tartly. "Would you really have shot him?"

"Yes, and the second barrel for that Corkscrew."

Bragg wheezed again, enjoying it all. "Some woman you got there, Toole. Wish I'd a had a woman like that one."

"Did young Apollo say anything?"

"No, Santo, the whole thing took less than a minute."

Tension and worry began to steal away from Santiago, and he slumped, weariness creeping through him. He'd have to go after them, with or without a posse. He pulled Mimi to him and hugged her, held her fiercely, his arms telling her things he couldn't express with lips.

"Oh, Santo," she whispered. "I was so afraid for you. That something bad had happened."

"It did happen, but Pericles got me out."

He held his wife, feeling her melt into him.

"Are there any patients?" he asked softly.

"Yes. The Stearn girl has a high fever. And Colonel Wade sent word that he wants to see you at once."

Irritation boiled through him. Wade never came to him; he always *sent* for him. Santiago sighed wearily. The Bragg outfit wouldn't get anywhere for a while. They had to cross the Yellowstone, and crossing over two thousand head would take a long time.

"I'd better go," he muttered. He would see Wade, and ask the post surgeon, Dr. Hoffmeister, to attend Sally Stearn. A doctor could do little to relieve a fever anyway. Mostly he could put a name to a disease and wait.

Mimi squeezed him tighter, not wanting to give up the comfort of his warmth. Then she let him go. "I don't like having Hermes Bragg here," she said. "He's an evil presence in our house. I wish I'd shot him. I'd have scalped him, too, and handed the scalp to that young lady."

"Tell that to him."

"I did. He roared and then started coughing again."

Santiago laughed. "In an odd way, I like

189

that scoundrel."

He let go of her reluctantly and slid into the summer kitchen, where Bragg's mocking eyes watched him. "Behave or my wife will scalp you," he said, and banged through the door.

Thirty minutes later he tied his big bay gelding to the hitch rail at the Fifth Infantry headquarters at Fort Keogh and strode lithely up the wooden steps.

"Ah, Sheriff, the army has something for you," Wade said, leering triumphantly. He always did that. Noblesse oblige. He corrugated his white forehead to give the impression of thought and studied the lengthy telegram before him. "Would you care to guess what it is?" he asked.

"Custer was discovered alive?"

"Close, close. I'll impart this information if you'll do us a favor, Toole."

Santiago waited calmly. Wade never gave information free.

"Arrest Little Lulu Belle and send her packing," Wade said, his eyes aglow.

"What did she do?"

"Why, give three officers an embarrassing disease, shortly thereafter contracted by their wives. It's kept Adelbert Hoffmeister busy, busy, and caused some distress here. I can't have distress. Not in my own bailiwick."

"That's not a criminal offense, Colonel."

"Well, think of something!"

"I'll propose treating her. Would that suffice?"

"No. She must be packed out."

"I'll encourage it, but I won't make false arrests, Colonel. Now what have you for me?"

Wade beamed. "Everything you wanted to know, Sheriff. Everything. The army has come to your rescue!"

"Why don't you just let me read that — "

"No, no, this is a confidential army communication, and it requires interpreting."

Santiago sighed and eased into a bentwood chair that did nothing to cushion his behind.

Colonel Wade steepled and unsteepled his hands and adjusted his rimless spectacles. "It's from the Pine Ridge Sioux agent via Fort Robinson. He's solved your case, Toole."

Santiago waited patiently, his mind upon the crossing of the herd some miles east of town. It'd take them all afternoon, he imagined. Tiredness tugged at him, but he tried to stay alert.

"Who'd you bury this morning, Toole?"

"Uh? Oh. Alonzo Montoya. One of Bragg's vaqueros. He died of mortification and blood poisoning of a leg wound."

"We see everything. I watched it with the

new field glass. We have a new field glass, Toole. I can see the flies Pericles Shaw shoots from here. I can see Mrs. Gatz hang her dainties in her bedroom. She won't hang them to dry out of doors, Toole. Did you know that?"

"Tell me," snapped Santiago.

"Ah, yes. It seems some of the Sioux herdsmen watching the tribal herd brought in a badly wounded man of theirs — gunshot, of course. The boy died. And another boy is in the post infirmary, also shot and dying. They wouldn't say what happened, but the agent finally wormed it out of them. They'd noticed two things — the trail of a large herd heading north between the southwest corner of the reservation and Fort Robinson, and a shortage in their own herd. They did a swift tally and came up a hundred and seventy-nine short. So they collected all the illegal Winchesters they had stashed somewhere — they're allowed side arms only, of course — and took off, fifteen of them, not telling the agent anything.

"The tracks were a week or so old. North a hundred miles or so they found a place where the herd had been stopped and animals probably branded. Fire ashes, a burnt cinch ring . . . They argued about it, some wanting to report it to the agent, some wanting to forge ahead and recover the stolen animals. If it meant a fight with whites, they vowed to keep it secret from the agent. Indians always get blamed, they figured.

"They caught up with Bragg on the Little Powder, Toole, maybe in your jurisdiction. They tried coming in with a white flag, to talk it over. They got close, maybe twenty, thirty yards, when Bragg, sitting in his wagon, yelled at his men to stop the Sioux. The fight got started that way. I take it the Sioux were prepared and returned fire faster than they received it, injuring Bragg's men, including the one you buried this morning. But they were beaten off, Toole, driven back without recovering their beeves. And they hid it all this time from the agent, fearing they'd be blamed for fighting with whites. But they couldn't hide the death and finally brought the wounded Sioux drover in."

Santiago sat silently.

"Aren't you going to say anything, Toole?"

"I'm filling in the rest," Santiago said softly. "Some of Bragg's drovers would have tried to stop the drive and separate the Sioux cattle that got sucked into the herd. No doubt Bragg — he's half-crazed with consumption and fever, Colonel — shouted at them not to, keep on going, keep on going. So they did, with some of them feeling plenty bad but still loyal to the brand, as they usually are. Same thing at the branding. Some hating it, hating what Bragg ordered them to do. Probably the segundo hated it, if I read him right. What's the Pine Ridge herd brand, Colonel?"

"IB, Indian Bureau, I think."

"That'd make an easy HB," Santiago said. "I saw some peculiar HBs. So they had their fight and brought a guilty secret with them. I suppose there's theft charges down there. Probably federal, since it's an Indian affair. I'll check with the United States marshal for Dakota. Are the Sioux drovers saying who shot at the Bragg outfit?"

"They all did."

"Probably justifiable homicide, given that they were shooting at robbers of almost two hundred beeves."

"You going to let those Injuns go scot-free after shooting whites?"

"Common law's always held a man's got a right to protect himself and his property, Colonel."

"That doesn't apply to redskins, Toole."

Santiago smiled. "The ones I'll charge are the drovers. They tried to defend their stolen goods. At least I'll charge them if this happened in my county. Starting with Bragg."

"You got strange notions, Sheriff. Get yourself laughed out of court by Pericles Shaw."

"We'll see. Thanks a heap, Colonel. Let me know if federal warrants are out on Bragg and the rest."

"Don't count on me for anything, Toole."

Santiago smiled and left, full of jangling thoughts.

Chapter 13

Santiago rode his big bay back to Miles City, scarcely aware of the trip, his mind lost in possibilities. Get warrants from Pericles Shaw. Raise a posse. Stop them before they escaped from the county. Warrants for whom? Six John Does, for jailbreak. No, make that seven. Almost certainly someone back at the Bragg camp held Jefferson Gonzales by force. Maybe more. Warrants for them all, for the death of a Sioux male on the Little Powder. A warrant for Hermes Bragg for ordering it. Maybe, if it happened in Wyoming, the warrants wouldn't stick. But they'd do, for the moment. Warrant for Athena Bragg, fugitive and conspirator in the jailbreak. The boss's daughter, able to stop it if she chose. And old enough to know the consequences.

Warrants. Too many to fit into the breast pocket of his frock coat. He'd need a posse. Not the army; the Posse Comitatus Act of 1878 forbade army assistance. Congress declared that the army could not participate in routine law enforcement; it could be called only for rioting, rebellion, or insurrection. Wade would refuse. Peace officers knew that soldiers were notoriously poor possemen and bound by rules anyway. The cavalry had regulations about ruining horses; outlaws didn't.

Where could he find twenty good men in a hellroaring camp like Miles City? He mulled a list of merchants, teamsters, saloon keepers, and street toughs, and realized he had poor pickings. He dismounted at Pericles Shaw's emporium and heard the explosion of the justice's revolver. Glass tinkled. Santiago's bay jerked back and broke the reins Santiago had just wrapped around the hitch rail. The sheriff cussed, briefly envying the drovers who'd taught their ponies to ground-hitch, and knotted the broken ends of the reins.

Then he stomped in. "Pericles, put that blasted revolver away! Look what you've — "

"Hold still," muttered Pericles, swinging the bore of his revolver straight past Santiago's breast, lining it up on a meandering yellowjacket. The explosion boomed. Sand blasted to the left. The bee flitted ahead.

"What were you saying, Toole?"

"I'll be glad when winter comes," Santiago roared. "No flies. And I'll sue you for deafness."

"Contempt of court. Two dollars."

"I want warrants."

"Dime each. Twelve for a dollar," said Shaw. "Court costs. Write them yourself.

I'll stamp my John Henry and you pay."

"Give me one blanket warrant for all parties, John Does, with the Bragg Cattle Company."

"Won't save money. I charge by the head."

Santiago dug in Shaw's rolltop desk, brushed sand off a fly-specked warrant form, and poked around for a nib pen. Nib pens were inventions of the devil, a blot on civilization. He found one, dipped it in gritty ink, and drafted his warrant. He could find no blotter so he waved it dry.

"Hold still," said Pericles Shaw.

Santiago saw the blistered barrel rotate in his direction and saw the yellowjacket hover just overhead.

"No!" he bawled, and ducked as the sand blew over him. The yellowjacket settled on his shoulder.

"No, Shaw!" he howled, bounding straight at the justice and tipping the mean revolver up.

"Contempt of court. Four dollars. Surrender yourself to the bailiff," yammered Shaw, laughing like a coyote over a carcass. He began pouring sand into cigaret papers and twisting the papers into small loads, while Santiago stared. The yellowjacket landed on Shaw's watershot maroon silk vest, and Santiago held his breath. Shaw finished loading hastily, slipped caps on nipples, and pointed his revolver into his gut, but the bee took off and drifted out a window.

"I'll sentence him to death," Pericles muttered.

Santiago found his bay a block down the street, dragging knotted reins and mincing sideways, looking back toward the source of the revolver shots. Muttering imprecations, Santiago caught his thoroughbred and rode back to his cottage.

Late afternoon. Where had the day gone? A burial, a jailbreak, imprisonment, release, a trip out to Fort Keogh, and a warrant, all in hours. His weariness caught up with him again, but his day had not ended. Patients to see. The evening rounds, which he'd neglected.

In his barn he slid tack off the bay, brushed the animal, hayed and watered him, and trudged wearily toward the whitewashed cottage, pondering his next move. Confront Bragg. The sheriff part of him demanded it; the doctor part of him worried that the confrontation might collapse Bragg's progress and send him to his doom.

He found Bragg resting quietly, awake and relatively free of the coughing. Santiago sat down beside the patient, took his pulse and temperature, examined his throat, and began his auscultation. He listened to the strange gurgle of ruined lungs and the thin arrhythmic beat of a worn-out heart. Bragg's bright brown eyes mocked the doctor, and he looked to be spoiling for some peculiar fun.

Santiago dropped his instruments back into the Gladstone.

"I imagine my herd's well nigh crossed the Yellowstone by now," Bragg mocked.

"Colonel Wade at Fort Keogh gave me the story. It came in on the military telegraph," Santiago began. "You want to add to it? Defend your actions?"

Bragg coughed happily. "Whatever be you talking about?"

"Theft of a hundred and seventy-nine beeves from the Sioux herd near Pine Ridge. Rebranding them a hundred miles north of there. Fighting the Sioux drovers down around my county line and killing — probably two."

Hermes Bragg laughed and then wheezed. "We made it to be a hundred and eighty-five. Them Injuns can't count, Toole."

"And two human lives."

"Injuns. They ain't human."

"I'm awaiting federal warrants, maybe a U.S. marshal in person, on the theft. As for the fight — "

"Self-defense, Toole. They were fixing to kill us."

200

"White flag and all, I'm sure. No, Mr. Bragg. I don't buy it. A jury might, since they don't convict a white man for killing an Indian. As you know. But I'll bring charges."

Bragg wheezed happily.

"I'm going to draft a note ordering your men to return to Miles City with the herd and themselves with it, along with your children. And I want you to sign it, Bragg. Then I'll go out and deliver it to Jefferson Gonzales and your children."

"I ain't inclined to sign. I want them up on the Judith, putting up a cabin and corrals and cutting prairie hay before the cold sets in. Why should I bring them back here?"

"To answer charges. Some fugitive charges might be dropped if you do it."

"No. If you haul the lot of them back, I'm not a-going to help none."

"Very well, Mr. Bragg. It'll go hard for your daughter and some of your men."

"No, I don't think so. This county's scarce organized and it'd take quite an outfit to whip mine. No, you'll fuss and fret and do nothing. You're soft, Toole. Doctor-soft. I've got your number."

There was something to that, Santiago knew. He doubted that the sheriff at White Sulphur Springs would be inclined to travel a hundred miles to tackle an armed, hardened cow-outfit, and eventually the whole trouble would die. Especially because it was Indian beef stolen and Sioux who were shot and killed.

"This the way you fixed it back in Texas?"

Bragg coughed and peered up with fever-brightened eyes. "A little different. I had to whup a few to show 'em who ran the county. You don't even need whupping, Toole. Sawbones don't need any whupping."

"You didn't answer my question the other day: Why is your crew loyal?"

"I'm a winner. Some fools call it winning in life's game, but Toole, life ain't a game. And I don't play. Some of them, they'd make a game of living and shrug their shoulders if they lost. I never made a game of anything, and if I lost I'd kill the winner."

"Let's try it again: why is your crew loyal?"

"Beats me. I'd kill 'em if they was otherwise."

"Were you good to them?"

"Hell, no. They get thirty and found, not forty. I shoot any I catch cheating on me. I run 'em hard from dawn to after dark. I bullwhipped a-plenty of 'em. I tell 'em if they don't like it, they can leave, and forget about drawing wages. They're slaves, them cowboys. Slaves of mine, Toole. And I use 'em as slaves because they ain't fit for more. Between them they haven't the brains to fit into a gnat's hind end."

"Why's Jefferson loyal?"

"Beats me. Worthless parasite."

"He told me he's got his own beeves in this herd."

"He thinks he does. Athena'll just humor him and do what she chooses with that brand, same as other brands."

"I don't believe you, Hermes Bragg. You bark but never bite. Except for women and children, of course. With the weaker ones and little ones, your bite was worse than your bark."

Bragg coughed violently, spraying sputum everywhere. "You make me sick, Toole."

"Sheriff Toole or Doctor Toole?"

"Both, dammit."

"Two things inspire loyalty, Mr. Bragg. Respect or love. Fear doesn't do it. Fear can produce outward submission, but not loyalty. Your men are genuinely loyal. So they either respect you or love you. I'd say, offhand, your children respect you and your crew loves you."

"Get out! Get out of here, Toole, before I kill you!" the man cried hoarsely, subsiding into coughing and a desperate gasping for air from lungs that wouldn't work. Bragg sucked and convulsed until Santiago thought he might die. But then the seizure slowly subsided, and Hermes Bragg settled flat on his back, staring up at Santiago with brimming eyes and tear-stained cheeks.

That evening Santiago heard the bawling of cattle across the river scarcely a mile from town and knew his quarry hadn't gotten far. They'd bed over there on bottom grasses that night and start driving west in the morning. He half expected a few drovers to swim their horses across that evening for a last hurrah in the west-end saloons.

He began his rounds with the determination to be thorough that evening. He took his Gladstone bag with him, planning to make three house calls en route. An oddity. A sheriff with a revolver bulging his black frock coat on one side and toting a medical bag with the other hand. Tonight he'd poke his head inside every dim saloon and check the bawdyhouse parlors as well, looking for any warm body from the Bragg outfit to toss in his pokey. If he could reduce their numbers, they'd become more tractable.

He walked north, to the riverbank, and spotted the amber campfire of the cow outfit across the river in cottonwood bottoms half a mile east of town, insolent in the night.

Good to know where they were, he thought. The cattle had settled to grazing and their lamentations had ceased. The good grass over there was a just reward for their passage through two hundred yards of mountain-cold water. Some of those cattle, he remembered, were stolen from the Sioux, from the United States government. Santiago stood in the dark, beneath clearing skies that popped stars and blanked stars with unseen windmills of black cloud. They would not get away. He felt his resolution taking hold and fueling his determination. He would bide his time if necessary, spring hard if necessary. But justice would be done.

Santiago looked up at the sky, watching stars vanish and reappear in the turbulent black. He couldn't do much for Hermes Bragg. Not as a doctor and even less as a sheriff. But if he could do anything, it'd be to help Bragg die in peace. Shrived, they said in the church. Santiago wished he didn't care. Let the old scoundrel die hard, ranting of his meanness. And yet, Santiago knew, he'd try to help Bragg. A man died only once, and every man hungered for a good death, unafraid, loved, and grieved at the moment of the loneliest passage of all.

Toole sighed and turned back into town. He walked quietly through a soft autumnal night toward Main Street, his eyes casing shadows, his free hand trying merchant doors, his eyes studying dark interiors for signs of furtive movement, broken glass, or disorder. He saw nothing amiss. Doctor and sheriff, keeping a wild frontier town healthy.

He cut south and knocked at the door of the Rock family. Granite Rock, a harness-maker, had named his boys Marble and Porphyry, and his girls Agate and Crystal. They took Santiago to Agate's room, where he examined the little girl by the yellow light of a kerosene lamp while Mrs. Rock hovered. He found fever, sore throat, and swollen neck glands. Her tongue had tiny red points over it. But what filled Santiago with foreboding was the vivid scarlet rash over the girl's whole body. A clear case of scarlatina, scarlet fever. He prescribed cool compresses to lower the fever, pleurisy-root tea, and liquid foods, such as broth or milk. And since scarlet fever was highly infectious, complete isolation from the other children.

"You just sleep and get well now, Miss Agate," he said too heartily. The child nodded.

"If she worsens, let me know at once," he said. He didn't tell them that the little girl had only a fifty-fifty chance and that he had precious little in his apothecary bottles to help her. He laved his hands and face carefully, using the pitcher and basin on the girl's washstand, wondering how many old-time doctors, ignorant of modern theories of sepsis and antisepsis, unwittingly spread disease with their unclean hands.

He stopped at the Gatz residence to have a look at Bernice's catarrh and then headed for his office at the jail, where he dropped off his medical valise. He didn't want to tackle saloon row toting a medical bag. Minutes later he was strolling easily through the tenderloin, looking for drunks in dark alleys — almost invariably cowboys or soldiers who'd been liquored up and rolled. He slipped around to the back of the saloons, looking for skulking footpads, bodies, anything and everything. Nothing tonight. He paused to study horses at hitch rails, noting brands carefully, looking hard for an HB or anything unfamiliar to him. Some of Bragg's drovers probably had ponies carrying their own Texas brand.

He never stayed long in a saloon, sensing that his presence put a damper on festivities. But on this night he paused long enough for a sarsaparilla. A quiet night. Scarcely a soldier and no cattle drovers. Only a few locals, eyeing him warily. It had grown too cold for the batwing doors of summer, so he pushed through plank doors into a wall of warmth as he poked into each place. In some laughter and talk died away, as it always did when the law hovered. In others, mostly cowboy places, the raucous good times seemed to intensify, and drovers made bets whether Santiago would buy himself a beer or stay dry. Tonight Santiago stayed dry.

He cased the brands on the horses at the parlorhouses and elected not to disturb the trade. He remembered his promise to Wade to talk to Little Lulu Belle but decided against it this night. Rounds done, and the sporting life in Miles City more or less calm, Santiago turned east on Main Street, heading for a night's sleep.

The lamplight in his sheriff's office caught his eye. He didn't remember leaving a lamp lit. He slid quietly toward the barred window fronting Main and peered in. Apollo. Teeth chattering, clothes dripping, bone cold. Santiago swiftly surveyed the rear of the building, finding a wet pony in the chill dark. No one else. That boy had risked pneumonia, swimming the cold Yellowstone at night to come here. Santiago trotted around to the door and burst in, startling Apollo.

"You'll catch a death of a cold, lad," he said gruffly, digging for a blanket.

"Sheriff Toole, I had to come." Wetness

filled the boy's eyes, and the sheriff knew it wasn't river water.

Santiago found a dirty jail blanket and threw it over the boy. "Now. Get out of those wet duds, lad."

A few minutes later Apollo Bragg huddled in a blanket beside a rapidly warming stove with a new fire catching in it.

"You want to talk to me, son?"

"Yes, sir. I got away, and Jefferson helped me. They think I'm asleep. Jefferson sent a message. He says, 'If you come, count on him.' "

Good news, thought Santiago. He'd read the man right.

"I came because I decided to. I'm going to tell you everything. Everything that happened starting at Pine Ridge. Even if it hurts my pa. I'm going to do what I think is right. And I told Jefferson Gonzales I was going to."

A prickly joy filled Santiago as he settled back in his desk chair, contemplating this young Bragg who'd become a man.

Chapter 14

The boy's shivering stopped when the office potbelly began to radiate heat. Santiago waited quietly behind his desk, a foot cocked upward. Apollo began hesitantly, stammering, seeking encouragement from Santiago with a boy's questioning eyes. Then his story began to flow, identical in all particulars with the report from Pine Ridge. They'd run into small groups of Sioux cattle dotting open range south of the reservation. Bragg's drovers had tried to drive them off but couldn't, as the great herd sucked more and more Pine Ridge longhorns into its long column.

Jefferson Gonzales had stopped a little north of the Sioux pasture and had started cutting out the Sioux beeves, a hard task without corrals handy. There was only a coulee to use as a containment. That went well but slowly, until Hermes Bragg, delirious with fever, awakened in his halted wagon. He clambered out waving two revolvers, and ordered the crew to proceed — with the Sioux beeves. Men stood silently. Gonzales tried to steer the consumption-crazed man back to his bed, quietly arguing with Bragg all the while. But Bragg yanked himself loose,

began driving bullets from his sixguns danger-
ously close to his own men. And then Athena
capped it: Do it, she said. Grumbling or
silent, the drovers released the Sioux cattle
they'd cut out, and the herd pushed north
once again, the joy gone out of the long
drive. Men turned somber and dour and
watched the trail behind them, waiting for
trouble to come. But it didn't. The Sioux
herders had been far away and the range
was vast and unfenced.

When Hermes stopped several days farther
along to rebrand, the boss of the Bragg Cattle
Company had slipped into wild, feverish shouting, intimidating men with his hollow, hoarse
yelling and endless revolver blasts. Some
branded. Some refused, wanting nothing to
do with it. The Bragg brands were HB and
AB, the former perfectly suited for running
iron work on the Sioux reservation IB brand.
Only one, the man called Corkscrew, seemed
to enjoy the labor. Most of the others worked
sullenly, loyal to the brand and yet doing
something dishonorable because old Bragg
and the ferocious girl insisted on it. Jefferson
Gonzales disappeared, his lips grim and jaw
clamped shut. . . .

Apollo proved to be a good narrator, Santiago thought, recollecting details and moods
with an adult eye. The further he slipped

into his long story, the better he became at it, remembering detail, remembering who resisted Hermes and his daughter and who took relish in rebranding.

They had finished their work and driven north again, still without the slightest sign of being followed, and some began to think the Bragg outfit would escape scot-free, trail and all, simply because the Sioux drovers never tallied their stock. But that was wrong. On the Little Powder, just inside of Montana Territory as they reckoned it from maps they'd gotten in Ogalalla, followers appeared, riding fast. Drovers they thought at first, noting the wide-brimmed hats, vests, chaps, and saddle-sheathed carbines. Drovers indeed, but darker than any they'd seen, most of them sporting braids of jet hair down their backs. The Indian cowboys had ridden past the drag while Bragg's men nervously checked revolvers. Past the flank and swing riders, heading toward point and the wagons that were ahead of the herd that day. Apollo and Athena watched them coming, a large group of Indians on wiry ponies. Apollo had felt afraid.

One among them rode with a white handkerchief tied to a stick, but all had carbines across their laps, ready to use. Outlawed Henry and Winchester carbines. The boy had hoped it would go easily, that the Sioux would be turned away. His father had taken the cattle, and there would be no turning back.

"That's how I felt then," he said to Santiago softly. "I don't feel that way now."

Santiago nodded.

But Hermes Bragg, feverish and crazed, hadn't even allowed talk to begin. He'd steadied his heavy revolver on the wagon gate and fired, a long pistol shot, but it hit the Sioux carrying the white flag. After that, chaos. Apollo and Athena both dove to the bed of the wagon and listened fearfully as carbines barked and men cried hoarsely. In only a minute it was all over. Three of Bragg's men had been shot. Some of the Sioux had been hit and rode off leaking bright blood.

"It seemed like a long time, but Jefferson said it lasted less than a minute," Apollo concluded.

The stove ticked as it heated. Santiago peered through the amber lamplight at the boy, letting whatever thoughts the lad had surface.

"I'm sorry," the boy cried, tears welling up.

"You were only a witness, lad."

"But I'm a Bragg! And I'm tattling on my father."

Santiago nodded gently. The boy looked utterly miserable, as if he'd betrayed a sacred trust. "There are many virtues, lad. Some more important than others. Your loyalty to your father is a fine thing. But you've seen a larger duty, lad. Truth and justice are more important."

Apollo's eyes leaked tears that slid down his smooth young cheeks. "I'm a Judas."

"I got the story from Colonel Wade, at Fort Keogh."

"I had to tell it."

"I know you did, lad. And you'll feel better for it. You've done a fine, manly thing. Something to be proud of all your life."

"I'm not proud of anything."

Santiago stared into the darkness, hoping he had the power to heal spirit as well as flesh.

"Tell me, son. What was your father like before he took the consumption?"

The boy contemplated the doctor's words. "We had a big white house with a covered porch on three sides to keep the sun off. It was hot there. And always sticky, sort of, except when we got a wind. My father always had men around him. Athena was the only girl. My mother — he sent her off."

"Did you miss your mother?"

"I won't talk about her."

The boy lapsed into silence and drew the blanket around him, staring at the orange dots of light around the stove door.

"He was always laughing. And the men laughed, too."

"What did they laugh about?"

"I don't know. Everything. Cow getting stuck in a bog hole. Cow having twins — that was a big joke. They'd find a slick calf on someone else's cow, brand it, and put it on one of our cows if she'd take it. We did it to them, and they did it to us."

"I guess your father's men liked him."

"Sure they did! He always joked with them. Hardly ever gave orders. When it came to branding and like that, he got right in with them and did the job. They got paid the same as anyone else, but he slipped them a few extras, like sending a barrel of beer over to the bunkhouse. He never could understand the outfits that acted strict and mean all the time. He just told the hands to have fun but not get careless."

"Did he talk tough? Say hard things against his neighbors?"

"He always talked like that. But when the bosses of the other outfits came over, they poured drinks and laughed, and sort of — insulted each other. He'd call one an old bandit, and they'd call him an old mossyhorn."

"What about that saying of his, if it breaks a leg, shoot it?"

"Oh, they all said that. They hardly ever did. Shoot it. Once Pa even put a splint on his favorite horse after it broke a foreleg in a gopher hole and then put it out in the river pasture. It was still out there when we left."

"I suppose what your father believed and what he did were two different things, eh?"

Apollo considered. "I never thought of it like that. He kept telling me and Athena we had to be hard, be tough, shoot broke-leg horses. He believed it. Sometimes he'd get mad at himself. He'd let a poor hand go, one who was worthless lazy or a petty thief, and he'd pay the man full wages and then stomp around the house, mad at himself, saying he should have booted the lazy man out without a dime because he didn't earn none."

The boy's wet clothing steamed near the stove. Santiago rose and turned them around, letting warmth reach the rear sides.

"Am I going to be arrested?"

"What for?"

The boy said nothing. "Is Pa going to be arrested?"

"He committed a crime."

"I want a direct answer!"

Santiago smiled. Bragg blood boiled through this lad. "There'll probably be federal warrants issuing from Dakota, and I imagine a U.S. marshal will come along soon. Theft of tribal property is a federal matter."

"What about the battle? Are you going to arrest him?"

Santiago peered into the young, worried face. "It doesn't seem to be self-defense, does it? Not with a white flag."

"You're going to arrest him."

"I don't know, Apollo."

The boy stared.

"Disease can derange a man. Fever can madden a sane man. Tell me, son. When did it all change? When did he seem different to you — not the pa you knew?"

Tears seeped from Apollo's eyes again and coursed down his cheeks.

"I don't know. It just happened so slow. He got to coughing down there, and taking fever, and getting mad. Then he took off for a while, clear to San Antonio. That's where he saw the doctors. They said consumption. They said it's a disease of the constitution, from miasmas of the air, especially damp air. Go where it's dry. And not so hot that a man's always sweating and every pond has miasmas rising from it."

"I suppose he began to change then."

"I guess so. He was always crabby. Nothing me and Athena did ever pleased him. He just sort of shouted all the time, and his coughing just got worse and worse. He put it off. For a long time, a year, he put it off and wouldn't do anything. And he'd go to San Antonio and the docs would tell him the miasmas were getting to him and he had to go somewhere far from south Texas. He got so hard to live with some of the hands quit. Jefferson Gonzales, he tried to talk — but Pa just got mad and coughed and told Gonzales to get out."

"I suppose you and Athena tried to help."

Apollo stared into space. "He thought we weren't hard enough. Not hard like him. He started preaching at us to be hard so when we took over we could keep our inheritance. He said — we'd lose everything . . . because we were soft like Ma."

The tears welled again, streaking Apollo's cheeks.

"Was your ma soft?"

"I don't know." The boy stared at the stove. "I wasn't very growed up when he made her go away."

"You miss her."

"I'm a Bragg! I don't miss nobody."

"My mother lives across the sea, in a green valley with a river running through it. I don't suppose I'll ever see her again. I can't go home, lad. I'd love to see her. She always had a kind word for me. She helped me become a doctor because she taught me to care about other people. She's well, last I heard. My father's gone, but she's well. You can go home, Apollo, and see your mother again, and find out all about her. I'd say she loves you."

"You can't go home? You did something bad?"

"Oh, yes, bad indeed. The youngest sons of peers cause difficulties just by being born."

"That's like me. I got born, and I haven't seen the end of it."

Santiago felt glad the boy hadn't asked him to explain the thing in England and Ireland that turned the younger sons of peers into outcasts, soldiers in India, or remittance men on the American frontier.

He poked at the boy's clothing and frowned. "Your things are still sopping. Would you like to stay in one of the cells — door open?"

"Please — the haunts will come."

Santiago smiled. "You mind walking a little in that blanket? I just happen to have some old long johns at home, about right for a boy who sleeps in the carriage barn loft. It's night; no one will see you walking. You can put your boots on. Dry, I see. You know the cowboy tricks crossing a river."

Apollo smiled and tugged the boots he'd hung from his neck when he swam the horse across the icy torrent. "I crossed just about every river there is," he said. "There's no bridges from here to Texas."

"You crossed the greatest river of all tonight, lad."

He settled the boy in the loft, deep in the hay, with two blankets for his chilled thin body. He wondered whether the drovers across the river would come in the night and kidnap the boy, but he doubted it. He slipped through the dark into his house and lit a lamp in his bedroom with a sulphur match. Mimi slept in her white flannel nightgown. The yellow light of the lamp turned her flesh umber. She didn't awaken and lay on her side, her lips slightly parted and her glossy black hair tumbling loose over her shoulders.

He turned the wick down, and as the lamp blued out he slid in beside her and pulled the covers up.

"Santo," she said in her sleep and nestled her head into the hollow of his shoulder. Her hand slid across his chest caressingly and she pulled herself close. He caught her in his arm and held her while she slept, enjoying her soft closeness in the night.

He didn't sleep. Faint starlight pierced the sash window, making a phosphorescent indigo square in the midst of blackness. Miles City, Territory of Montana. What an alien place for an Irishman to be, he thought. Stranger still were his two vocations, which had been pulling at him and tearing something within him more and more. Once in a while they formed an alliance within him but mostly they warred, as they did now about the fate of the Braggs.

A person dedicated to medicine should do nothing else, nothing at all but heal the sick and save lives, he thought. He should read every journal, master every advance of knowledge, learn specialties. He should return to Europe and study with surgeons, learn the pathology he never learned, master the anatomy he'd never mastered. He'd studied under Lister; now it was time to study under Koch, if Koch in Germany would have him.

Troubled, he stared into the gloom, comforted by the quiet breathing of the woman he loved nestled into him. He'd drifted like a tumbleweed to the little town rising around Fort Keogh and begun a practice that netted him almost nothing. A few dollars, assorted chickens, saddles, a dray horse, and a lot of promises. Not enough. Mimi came to him one day, carried south from her mother's people in a litter because she was far gone with typhoid fever. Her abdomen distended with rose spots on it; her fever was 105 degrees. Her mouth and tongue were caked with a dirty brown crust. She'd fallen into a delirium, muttering incoherently. He nursed her through, with a little more than cold compresses that lowered her fever to 103, and gave her moments of peace and all the juices and broth and water he could force into her. It took a month, but slowly she returned from the dead.

He tried to ignore all the things doctors are supposed to ignore, her tall, slim, golden beauty, her angular face with its high cheekbones, her great soft eyes that followed him. And as she healed, he discovered her St. Louis convent schooling, her French, her wry good humor. And her love. There being no priest in Miles City, they did not wait for the benefit of the clergy.

He hadn't sought the sheriff job; it came to him shortly after the town merchants had organized a county and the territorial legislature had agreed to it. They needed a sheriff and found no one suitable among the roving buffalo runners, saloon keepers, or bawdyhouse owners who camped in Milestown for the duration of the boom. Would the under-employed doctor perform the honors temporarily, until a real lawman could be found? Santiago examined his flat purse and the new burden of caring for Mimi and assented.

The town fathers had discovered, to their amazement, that the Irish doctor knew how to stop brawls, could cold deck a man larger than himself, and could fire a bullet into the ace of spades. The temporary sheriff had become the permanent one. But Santiago knew that someday soon he'd quit. More and more lawing tore at him. How could a man passionately dedicated to healing face a killer like Corkscrew, shoot or be shot? How could a man dedicated to healing even someone as far gone as Hermes Bragg arrest him and condemn him to instant death in a cold jail? How could he arrest and send to jail a young lady, not yet in womanhood, whose father had brutally twisted her mind? Once in a while it worked the other way, too. He'd healed loathsome scum doomed to jail or hanging, giving medicine to criminals who deserved their bullet holes and disease. Sometimes his medical practice had led him to crimes, to women who'd been assaulted, men who had been shot by bandits, Indians who'd been tortured by whites, starved orphan children who'd been enslaved by teamsters and plowmen. Many cases were like that, where the healing took both his medicine and his power to stop or punish crime.

"What are you thinking, Santo?" Mimi asked dreamily.

He didn't answer but drew her closer as she burrowed into his shoulder. He felt the silk of her hair on his neck.

"You're thinking about moving away."

"Maybe I could practice where there's more patients," he ventured. "Maybe Helena or Butte." He'd thought of that many times, but his thoughts always returned to Mimi. Taking her away from the northern plains, taking her away from her mother's people. Taking her somewhere that would accept her half-Indian blood even less than people here accepted it.

"You're thinking about the Braggs. Whether to be a doctor or a sheriff. It's often like that, Santo. Don't be torn apart."

"I'd like to study surgery. Not be just a country doctor."

She rolled over and kissed him. "You'd like not to think about the Braggs."

He had to admit it was true.

Chapter 15

The hammering on his door rattled culture dishes and skulls in his office, sent the tiger-striped cat scurrying into a closet, and precipitated dust from the swaying chandeliers. Santiago muttered, glanced at the turnip watch beside his nightstand, and tugged himself out of a sensuous languor. Six twenty-five, ten minutes after the eastbound Northern Pacific passenger train had wailed him partially awake.

He strapped his black revolver belt over his nightshirt and made for the rattling door. A sheriff matter. No one seeking a doctor awakened the dead like that. Just before the door splintered off its hinges, he opened it, peered into a poised fist the size of a boulder, and then beyond it to a graying man built of granite.

"Sheriff Toole?"

Santiago nodded mutely, wondering how granite could be fitted to herringbone and leather patches at the elbow.

"I'm Lucullus Handy, deputy U.S. marshal, Helena office."

"Ah," said Santiago. "I thought maybe you sell tombstones."

The marshal eyed him suspiciously from hot black eyes that could inflict pain on whatever they gazed upon. "We have business."

"I suppose we do," muttered Santiago. "Sit in here while I dress."

"No time for dressing." The man bulled in, his gaze shattering skulls and intimidating the microscope. "What's all this — evidence? Skulls. Skeleton. Plain murder. Are you a lab man? They're the coming thing, lab men."

"Physician."

"Sawbones! Sawbones! I'm looking for the sheriff, Toole."

"That's me."

Handy eyed him sulphurously. "I don't believe it. I travel by bouncing stage from Helena clear to Livingston, catch a train at the railhead, whip here on urgent business, and the sheriff turns out to be a mick doc in a nightshirt."

"Have a seat," said Santiago wearily. "And don't disturb my specimens."

He made to leave, pull some pants on — he never cottoned to sheriffing in a nightshirt — but the marshal roared at him.

"No, you don't. Every second counts. We'll nail the bums."

Santiago paused and then sank into the swivel chair behind his cluttered desk. His revolver poked him in the kidney, so he shifted it and then finally unbuckled his belt and laid it on his desk, dropping the holster so the Remington's barrel pointed at this source of dawn torment.

"I have warrants," Handy said. "We'll nail 'em."

"Who for?"

Handy looked surprised. "For that Bragg outfit. The ones you got in custody. Every last one."

"I don't have any in custody."

Handy drilled him with a glance that could have lit a sulphur match. "You let them go?"

Santiago sighed. He hated to admit it. "I had one in custody, but she broke out."

"She . . . broke . . . out."

"That's correct."

"She."

"Bragg's daughter, Athena. She's fourteen."

"Let me get this straight. A girl busted jail, and you haven't nipped the rest?"

Santiago nodded, suddenly irked.

"Are you really the sheriff? You got a brother or something?"

Santiago nodded. Handy tugged at his walrus mustache while his eyes blinked methodically. Handy seemed methodical down to eye-blinking.

"How come they don't have a real lawman?"

227

Santiago felt miffed. His record stood up better than that of most lawmen, but he knew it made no difference. Prejudice was prejudice.

"Ask the county commissioners."

Handy's gaze dismissed Toole as morticians dismiss the healthy and young. "Never mind. I'll handle it myself. Where's Bragg?"

"In bed in my summer kitchen."

Handy blinked again, shuttering his bearded gaze. Santiago felt as if he'd been tintyped and frozen in Handy's rogues' gallery. "Well, at least you've got him nabbed. How come he's not in the county lockup? You and him are pals, maybe?"

"He's dying of consumption. I'm treating him."

"Treating him! Why are you treating a felon?"

Santiago smiled wanly. "I presume you are referring to Bragg and not an abscess of the finger. I don't know that Hermes Bragg's a felon. I don't believe he's been convicted of it."

"Anyone steals a hunnert seventy-nine cows is a felon." Handy dug in his tweed coat for a sulphur match and began cleaning his fingernails with the wooden end. Then he extracted a long green Havana from his breast pocket, bit the butt, placed the fingernail-cleaner match in an ashtray, and sucked the unlit cigar. "I don't smoke," he said. "But I like the taste. And if I wipe a bed tick with it, the bedbugs stay away. If I fire it up, the women stay away."

The man had it in for bedbugs, women, and felons, Santiago thought.

"Where are the rest? The stolen beeves?"

"Across the river. On bedground there until this morning. I imagine they started up at daybreak."

"You're letting them go?"

"No. Gathering evidence."

Handy beetlebrowed a moment, whipped out a piece of foolscap and a pencil, and wrote something. "I think you're in cahoots," he said. "Letting them go."

"Mr. Handy. Would you mind telling me how many miles a herd of two thousand-some cattle make in a day? And how many miles a horseman can make in a day?"

"I think you're in cahoots."

Santiago shrugged. He felt unequal to the interrogation dressed in his white nightshirt.

"You don't deny it, I see."

"I deny it."

"Well, at least you got Bragg here. I'll throw him in the county lockup, and you'll give me the key."

"No, you won't. Even moving him from

here to there's likely to kill him."

"Well, that's what we want! He killed some Injuns, didn't he?"

"That has yet to be determined, Mr. Handy."

"You're in cahoots."

"I'm in a nightshirt."

"Get dressed then. I'll go nip Bragg and haul him over to your lockup."

"No."

"What do ya mean, no? That's what I came to do and that's what I'm going to do."

"He's not going anywhere. Too weak even to get out of bed. And under my medical supervision. You kill him and I'll file manslaughter charges."

Handy grinned, his gummy cigar pushing erect. "Try it. Try nipping a marshal performing his duty."

"You have a choice of hastening a man's death or not."

"If he's dying, what do you care? So he dies a day early. You must have cut a deal."

"Three times now you've accused me of violating my oath of office. Be careful with your tongue; it might get you in trouble. My profession is to save lives. And my Hippocratic oath is to do no one harm. Actually, he's rallied enough so that I'd give him a few months."

"Some sheriff."

"All right then, Mr. Handy. Arrest him and leave him in his bed, in my custody. If he escapes, I'm liable as a lawman."

"Nuts to you, mick. Where is he?"

"What do you plan to do?"

"Walk the felon to your jail."

"Consumption is contagious. I've treated families in which the children died one by one, each getting it from the others."

"Bull. You wouldn't have him here."

"I wash with a mild antiseptic after each examination. I'd suggest that you do, too."

"Bull. I'd never take consumption. I'm built like an oak. If he can't walk I'll drag him by the belt."

"If that doesn't finish him, that cold stone jail will. If you have to take him, rent a dray from the livery barn."

Handy guffawed. Santiago felt tempted to slide the Remington from its nest on his desk and point it.

"All right, before you lace your corsets and pull on your petticoats, Toole, let's get the rest of this. How many drovers do I nip over there?"

"Six or seven."

"Toole, it wasn't six or seven drovers that ran a mess of longhorns clear up from Texas."

"Eighteen. Most had no part of the theft,

231

rebranding, or fight with the Sioux. As for the fight, most of the drovers were back on drag or flank or swing and not up front where it happened. As for the theft, most of the crew tried to cut out the Sioux cattle. As for the rebranding, most of the crew took a walk, including the segundo. I'm sorting them out."

"My warrant says all, right down to the cook." Handy waggled his green cigar and sandpapered Toole with his gritty gaze. "Them that didn't actually do it were accomplices even so."

That was probably the case, Santiago thought. Loyalty to the outfit. Nip them all, and let the federal courts sort it out.

"I'd like the children placed in my custody."

"No one's staying in your custody — Sheriff."

"The children were under duress — a tyrannical, crazed father. It serves no public good — "

"Then why did you put little Miss Bragg in jail?"

Santiago sighed. "Shooting at me. Thwarting my investigation of brands."

Handy chortled cynically. "Some children. The girl sounds like innocence itself. Naw, Toole, this warrant says all, and I'll nip all. Even little sheriff-shooting ladies. How'd she bust out?"

"Six or seven of the drovers sprung her when I was bringing her back from a burial."

"A burial now! You took her to a burial!"

Santiago tired of it. "I'll shave and dress," he said, sliding up from his desk.

"You do that and I'll nip old man Bragg while I wait. Shove some duds on him."

The man built of granite plunged through the cottage as if he owned it, bulled into the kitchen and out upon the porch. Straight past Mimi, who stood at the bedroom door in her wrapper, her eyes dark and Indian.

From out in the summer kitchen he heard violent paroxysms of coughing and knew he was listening to murder. Then the bawling of an ulcerated larynx, and the easy rumble of federal authority. Then Bragg's crazed laugh, which collapsed into terrible sucking and gasping.

Santiago toyed with the belt and holster in his hand, feeling the weight of the shining black Remington. Rage. Hot anger. A wall of lava burning through him, eating everything. The sounds out there got his Irish up until he could scarcely breathe. Mimi watched him, knowing well what could explode inside him.

"Santo — "

Santiago Toole looked at the drawn Remington in his sweated hand and felt a wall of Irish fire subside slowly. He knew he had come closer to murder than he'd ever come in his life. The murder of a federal lawman making a legitimate arrest. He'd never thought of himself as a murderer before. He leaned against the doorjamb, staring numbly at the weapon, realizing that he, too, could commit the darkest crime. Holy Mary, he thought.

He slid the weapon back, decided against a shave, and raced to put on his duds. The faster he got Bragg settled in jail with several blankets and some belladonna to slow down the spasms, the better the chance that Bragg's rally might continue. But even as he yanked up his britches over his nightshirt and buttoned them, he knew. He'd heard murder.

He buckled his black gunbelt on and raced to the summer kitchen. Empty. He pushed out into the yard. Empty. He ran to the street. Ahead a block, Handy dragged Bragg toward the county jail, one of Handy's massive arms holding up a man too weak to walk. Bragg wore britches and nothing else, and his bare feet scraped along frosted earth.

Santiago realized he carried the wrong thing: he didn't need his gunbelt, he needed his Gladstone bag. He sprinted back to his office and snatched it up and went out again. A glimpse of Apollo, gawking at the barn door, stopped him. The boy looked terrified.

"Apollo! You run into the kitchen, lad. Mrs. Toole will feed you."

Mimi, still in her wrapper, stared out the back door.

"They took Pa!"

Santiago paused. "Just to the jail, lad. I'll get him settled there."

"They're going to get me!"

Santiago didn't know how to answer. He was not given to lies, even comforting ones. "I'm fighting it," he said at last.

Apollo looked stricken. He stood at the barn door, wearing an old union suit of Santiago's. His duds were still at the jail, drying.

"Apollo, you come in now," said Mimi.

But the boy's cheeks shone with wetness. He gawked a moment longer and then ducked into the barn. Moments later the boy bolted out of the barn on his mustang cowpony, a skinny lad in a union suit racing his pony toward the river.

"Apollo, lad, don't!" cried Santiago.

Too late. The boy steered his pony north to the river, past several homes, and disappeared into masses of brush along the bank.

Santiago watched with a sinking heart. The

federal marshal may have murdered not one but two Braggs.

He walked swiftly to Main Street and then west toward the lockup and his office, fuming and ready to throw the marshal himself into the pokey.

When he entered his office he found Handy hunting for a key. Back in the cellroom Bragg sprawled on the cold rock floor of a cell, unconscious and sucking air.

"Don't you meddle, Toole," snapped Handy. "I should throw you in there, too. Where's the key?"

"Find it yourself," snapped Santiago. He pushed through to the cellroom and lifted Bragg up to the hard wooden bench that served as a cot. He found the barest thread of a pulse, erratic and fast, pausing alarmingly. Bragg's body felt icy, the kind of cold that prefaces death. He grabbed a filthy blanket and covered the man, gently tucking it around Bragg's icy, naked feet.

Bragg sucked and gasped.

"I said where's the key?"

"This man is dying," retorted Santiago. "What do you need a key for?"

"You've already had one Bragg busted out," growled Handy. With that he lifted Santiago bodily from behind and dug a massive hand into Santiago's pockets, coming up with coins, a pocketknife, and no key. He dropped Santiago in a heap.

Santiago's rage flared and he swung around, ready to show the federal hunk of beef a thing or two about brawling, and then remembered he had a dying man to save if he could. The doctor in him won again, and he began rummaging in his bag for powders.

But Handy's paw caught him from behind and sent him sprawling again. "Where's the key, Sheriff?"

From the cold stone floor Santiago sorted through wildly conflicting impulses.

"Do I have to pound you, too?" snapped Handy. "Some sheriff."

"Around somewhere," he muttered. In fact Pericles Shaw had one set and the drovers who broke out Athena had the other. "Go look for it. I'm busy. This man's dying. You may have killed him."

Handy stared at Bragg. "Save a trial," he said, and lumbered out to the office. Santiago heard the sound of crashing drawers.

Dr. Toole eyed his patient gently. Bragg no longer convulsed in paroxysms of uncontrolled coughing. His heart was failing. Maybe foxglove. He uncorked the bottle of foxglove extract and applied two drops, a minimum dose, to Bragg's tongue. He waited in the cold gloom.

"You've hidden the key on me, Toole," yelled Handy. "What kind of jail is this? Where's your turnkey?"

"County can't afford a full-time one," replied Santiago. "I'm the turnkey."

"Where's your deputy?"

"I have none."

"Where's your magistrate?"

"Next door."

"He'll have a key. I know how these towns work."

Handy plunged out.

Bragg's rapid, thready pulse slowed and strengthened. Santiago laid his stethoscope to Bragg's trembling chest and heard the change. He pressed it to Bragg's left lung and listened to the terrible gurgle made by air rushing past the massed tubercules that had built up within.

"You lost, Toole." Bragg's rasping voice startled Santiago. The man coughed and laughed until he capsized into silence again.

Santiago drew back, out of the infectious spray of Bragg's mouth. "Mr. Bragg, I think we can keep your rally going — if you want to live."

Bragg laughed.

The man had turned feverish. Santiago found heat in Bragg's forehead, and the hot, bright eyes told of deepening trouble. He stared dourly at Bragg, sensing the future.

"I'll be back. You might save yourself if you want it enough. If not, you might think upon your foolish life and make peace with your abused children and God and the law. It's the best way to die."

Bragg peered up at him quietly.

Santiago stood. He'd have to arrange for jail meals again with Chang Loon. But not for long, he thought. He'd walk home now, something of a spectacle: nightshirt, britches, hightop shoes, and unshaven. But the day had barely begun, and everything in it would be governed by a U.S. deputy marshal who reminded him of tombstones.

Handy bowled in, looking stormy. "No one there."

"It's not yet seven."

"Where does he live?"

Santiago sighed. "Mr. Handy, you just sit here and guard the dangerous felon back there. The drovers who broke out his daughter have one key ring and the justice, Pericles Shaw, has the other. He's not going to surrender it to you. I'll be sending a Chinaman in with food for you and Bragg — if Bragg wants any. I'll be in and out, attending Bragg. If you lock me or the Chinaman out, I'll press my own charges."

Handy settled himself into Toole's desk

chair. "I'll just do that. No prisoner's ever gotten away from me."

"Fine, fine, Marshal. I'm going to dress, breakfast, and look in on a case of scarlet fever. You guard the felon."

Chapter 16

He went home to ready himself for the day. All the while he shaved and dressed he pondered that federal marshal sitting in his jail house. Nothing had come to Santiago, no plan at all, as he snapped a fresh starched collar to his white shirt, pulled himself into it, tugged on his black vest with its star, and squirmed into his frock coat. In Ireland and Scotland he'd have hung a cravat to his neck, but here he couldn't quite force himself to it, except for funerals and hangings. He wolfed a bowl of oatmeal while Mimi watched silently, well aware that Santiago's mind ran far away that hour. From his breakfast table he made straight for the Rocks, to attend Agate.

Agate Rock's condition had deteriorated. The slender little girl's heart pattered and thumped in her small chest. Fever raged through her, and Santiago measured it at 104 degrees. He pondered the child, who lay hot and scarlet, her coverlet thrown off. So little he could do. Foxglove. He'd had some success with it, and so had other physicians. A tricky thing, though. He eyed the child, guessed at sixty pounds, and decided on a single drop of the extract in water. She had trouble swallowing it and tumbled back. He waited and then applied his stethoscope. Slower beat. He waited again, noting that the red flush lessened somewhat.

He turned to Camille Rock. "Cool compresses now, steadily over the next hour. I want that fever broken. Lowered, anyway." He smiled gently. "I think she's going to make it. She's a strong child."

She nodded. "Will you stay?"

He sighed and shook his head. "A lot of urgent things today. I'll be close, though. My office or the sheriff's office. If I'm forced to leave, I'll send word to Dr. Hoffmeister at the fort."

"That's too far away — "

Santiago nodded unhappily. "See how that flush has lessened. If it returns, fetch me. If her heart starts racing, fetch me."

He didn't want to leave, and they didn't want him to. He snapped his Gladstone shut and trotted silently down the stairs on a purple runner pinned by carpet rods. Granite Rock had already left for work, but the children stared silently as he passed them.

It occurred to him on Main Street that he had no plan. He had trouble organizing his thoughts. A herd pushing west, toward the county boundary. Bragg in jail, dying again. Apollo . . . dripping wet no doubt and running his pony up the wide, trampled swath behind the herd. Athena, who participated in her own jailbreak. Good men and bad with the herd, most of them innocent more or less; a few of them culpable. Jefferson Gonzales, probably an ally out there. Lucullus Handy, a rock-hard federal marshal with the power to arrest every last one of them. Santiago juggled all of this, perplexed, and came to no conclusions at all.

He found no one in his office. The silence startled him. He'd expected the room to be filled with the flinty presence of Handy occupying the chair behind Santiago's desk. But the office lay cold in the early light. From next door he heard the muffled booms of Pericles' revolver. Handy probably had found a café and was chowing down. Even granite-brained marshals needed breakfast, he thought.

The cellroom door lay open and unlocked, so Handy hadn't dug a key out of the justice. Santiago walked into the cellroom and into the wall of cold, ancient urine and other undecipherable odors that resulted from fear, duress, disease, hangovers, and neglect. He could smell hate in that lockup. He'd always sworn hate reeked.

He found a lamp and scratched a match,

lighting the wick. He carried it through the gloom to the cell where Bragg lay, the same cell in which Montoya had died. He held the lamp over Bragg and saw the man peering up at him from fevered eyes. In the space of two or three hours, Bragg had changed. On the summer kitchen cot, Bragg had seemed vital, wrestling against death. His emaciated, sunken body somehow resisted the last onslaught of the advanced consumption. But here . . . Santiago sensed the change at once, staring down at the man. His flesh lay like white parchment over his bones. His eyes had sunk deep into his skull until they formed dim windows in the bottom of dark caverns. His lips had become bloodless and dry.

Santiago sat at the edge of the bunk and grasped Bragg's hands. They were cold. He reached for Bragg's feet and found them icy, along with Bragg's ankles. The dwindling heat of the living had retreated to the man's torso. Bragg's gaze followed Santiago, but other than that he showed no life at all. No coughing, no spasms. Santiago's stethoscope revealed a barely discernable pulse. He sighed, putting away his instruments. Only the waiting remained.

"Dr. Toole." Bragg's voice rose whispered but clear to Santiago. "I'm going now." He said nothing for a while. "You gave me some hope back there at your house. A gift of a few months. I got to liking it."

Bragg lay inert on his back, some faint, irregular rhythm lifting his lungs and lowering them. Santiago took the man's cold hand into his own.

"Didn't take much to destroy the hope, did it. A short walk with a U.S. marshal." Bragg spoke quietly. "You said a man could die well or die badly; die right or die wrong."

Santiago listened and waited.

"I don't know about God. If he exists, I still don't know about heaven. Or afterlife. If that exists, I don't suppose I've got much claim on His pasture. But if He's listening, I guess I'll say I didn't live right, didn't do it right."

Santiago listened intently. He'd heard more deathbed confessions than a dozen priests together, and they never failed to touch something within him.

"I hurt Clarissa — my wife. Hurt her bad." Bragg stopped there and stared up into the gloom until Santiago thought that he'd finished with the subject. "Tell her I'm sorry I hurt her. In San Antonio. Too late now. She never did me no harm, but I took her wrong . . . I can't explain it. Too worn out."

245

Santiago nodded.

"I got my boy and girl into trouble. Taught the wrong things. You've got to fix them up, Toole. You tell them I said I was wrong. I wish they was here, and I could tell it myself. I think the girl's plumb ruint, but maybe the boy, he'll pull through. You tell them — you tell them — " Bragg blinked his eyes slowly. "You tell them I — you know what I mean."

"Love?"

"Oh, don't get notions like that. Tell them I got to thinking — I got to feeling that — oh, hell, Toole, tell them what you think."

Santiago cleared his throat. "I'll tell Athena and Apollo that you loved them."

Bragg glared at him. "They'll say you're lying."

"Am I?"

Tears formed in Bragg's dry eyes.

Santiago waited. Bragg couldn't come to grips with anything tender, even when he tried. "I'll tell them," he said at last.

"You tell the rest that I did wrong and got them into trouble. My last wish is that the Sioux beeves be cut out and returned plus a few more to balance the scales."

"I'll tell them."

"You keep Jefferson Gonzales out of it, the charges. He fought me, told me I done

246

wrong, got mad at me." He managed a weak grin. "Don't suppose you can help much with that Handy."

"I'll try."

"I got a lot more, bad stuff. I killed men. I put my brand on everything that had four legs, mine or not . . . I'm getting tuckered out talking, Doc."

"You rest then."

Santiago waited while Bragg closed his eyes and seemed to slide into some distant land. But then Bragg opened his eyes again.

"Are you a believer?"

"I am."

"You think you can pray me out of this jackpot?"

"I believe God hears prayers and is merciful."

"Pray for Bragg, Toole."

Hermes Bragg closed his eyes again and seemed to relax. Santiago waited, observing some subtle change as the man's features softened. The man had given up contact with the living and slid slowly toward the final coma. Even Bragg's cold hands felt loose as death now. His breath came in soft, irregular gusts, and Santiago supposed death would come soon, in minutes or hours.

Santiago sat in the chill cell, waiting for death. He would stay. No man deserved to die alone. Not Hermes Bragg. Not even Lucullus Handy. As he sat, he tried to form some sort of prayer but couldn't. He didn't grieve for this old renegade, but he found himself admiring Bragg for a lot of things, including his last thoughts and words.

He wouldn't leave. He wouldn't let go of Hermes Bragg's cold hand. Bragg would somehow know if he let go and would die alone. He sat beside the comatose man, trying to make sense of the frontier and the flinty hardness it had spawned out of necessity. Men who roamed west of the law and west of order and west of love and west of God did what they had to. Some had been ruined by it, twisted into something brutal and dark. As if God had drawn his deadline down the Mississippi River.

Distantly he heard the street door slam and the stomp of boots on his wooden office floor.

"Toole, are you in here?" roared Marshal Handy.

"I'm here."

"So dark in here I can't see. Some jail."

Handy bulled into the cell and stared.

"He's dying," said Santiago. "You killed him."

"Bull. I'm a marshal, and I put a felon in the pokey."

"It's not as simple as that."

"I got a set of keys, but now I don't need it. That Shaw. Some card. We shot flies for an hour. I got three bees. Come along, Toole. We'll ride out to that herd and nip the whole lot of them."

"I'll come along presently. I'll stay with Mr. Bragg until he passes."

Handy glared at him. "Neglecting your duty. You're some sheriff."

"Doing my duty," retorted Santiago stubbornly. "Go ahead if you want. You've got federal warrants."

"I want some backup. I can handle any ten boneheaded drovers, but eighteen might get notions."

"No man should die alone. Not even you, Handy, even though you deserve it."

"Dammit, Toole, he doesn't even know you're there."

"Perhaps you're right. But I'm sticking."

Handy glared. "I want a horse. And I'll saddle one for you."

"You can sit over there and wait like a decent man. And while you wait, I'll tell you a little of what Mr. Bragg said on his deathbed. He exonerated some. The segundo of the outfit, Jefferson Gonzales, fought him all the way, refused to help steal cattle, refused to rebrand, and walked out."

"A Mexican," said Handy. "Very interesting."

"You just sit there and pay your respects. If you have any respect in you. Your head is full of disrespect."

Handy grinned maliciously. "I ought to pull you out of here at gunpoint, Toole."

"Go ahead. Shoot Doc Toole and tell the world I was resisting arrest."

"I don't hear you calling yourself sheriff."

Santiago stared into Bragg's face. The mouth had fallen open. Santiago pulled a small pocket mirror from his Gladstone and held it to the man's nose and mouth. It steamed slightly. Life threaded on.

"You'll hear it shortly, Handy. I'm going to ride out there alone. I don't want you along."

The marshal grinned malevolently.

"Hermes Bragg left messages with me a few minutes ago. I'm to deliver them to his children and his crew. If I do so, I believe they'll return here without resistance. I'd just as soon do it by myself."

Handy laughed. "Secret messages. I suppose the old scoundrel told them to come in and face the music. No, Toole. I've got the lay of the land here. You need someone along to prop up your backbone when it starts to bend."

"Pound him, Toole," said Hermes Bragg.

Santiago whirled and stared. The man lay moribund, mouth open, face white, flesh icy.

"Jesus," said Lucullus Handy. The marshal let himself down slowly on the opposite bunk and watched, his eyes blinking methodically again.

Santiago watched, too. Watched the spirit take flight, the body ease slightly. Hermes Bragg had died. Santiago had encountered the thing before, comatose people speaking clearly at the last and then slipping away. He held up his mirror and got no moisture. He pulled out his stethoscope and found no rhythm, only the soft sighing of escaping gases, like a teakettle taken off the stove.

"He's gone."

Handy nodded.

Santiago turned his back on the marshal and prayed. Then he stood quietly. In his office he filled out forms. Out on the street he trudged toward Sylvane Tobias's cabinetwork shop, scarcely aware that Handy had shaken himself loose and had tagged along. He found Tobias sipping tea and working his accounts.

"One more box, Sylvane."

The cabinetmaker peered up over half-glasses.

"Hermes Bragg. You can measure him at the jail."

"The old man himself, eh? County or private?"

Santiago thought. "Private," he said at last. "I'm fetching that crew back."

"You sure they're going to — "

"No, I'm not."

"Pine plank, then."

"No, Sylvane. Make it hardwood and fine."

"But if they don't — "

"If they don't, I'll lay Marshal Handy here in it. Make it long enough for Handy."

The marshal eyed Santiago sulphurously but said nothing.

"I suppose you'll want a hole — "

"Yes, next to the two drovers we buried."

"Toole! I can't do that. Bragg isn't Mex. He's a white man. Was he a Mason by any chance?"

"Next to the two drovers, Sylvane."

Tobias glared back defiantly. "Over my dead body."

"And harness Heaven," Toole added acidly.

"Heaven! He deserves Hell and no other! Stealing cattle — even if it was from Injuns. Killing Injuns . . . Well, maybe Purgatory. Killing Injuns don't count."

"Heaven, Tobias. Bragg sought his maker before he died."

"I don't think I'm following this," said Handy. "But I'm inclined to nip it in the bud."

"Our friend here thinks he's St. Peter," muttered Santiago. "Or at least privy councillor to St. Peter. He's got three drays, speckled white, gray, and black, named appropriately."

"Make it Hell, Tobias," said Handy. "Deathbed reforms don't count."

"Somebody'd better pay. Who'll do the preaching?"

Santiago fixed the marshal with his eye. "Handy, here."

"Why me, Toole?"

"You killed him; you bury him. His children will profit, no doubt."

Handy glared.

"You stay here, Handy. If I go alone, I can bring them back peacefully. I'll leave directly and be back tomorrow with most of them, excepting a handful watching the herd. No need to bring the whole herd back. We'll cut the stolen beeves after the burial."

"I have warrants to serve, Toole."

Santiago sensed that Handy wouldn't budge, wouldn't even consider any other plan. More blood, then. "I can't stop you, Handy. But if you go, we should enter their camp unarmed."

"Are you crazy, Toole?"

"I'd better make more boxes," said Sylvane Tobias.

"Drovers live by a code, Handy. You're not dealing with miners or outlaws or teamsters. You're dealing with a certain breed, a Texas breed . . ."

"I'm taking a double-barreled scattergun and two Colts," rumbled Handy.

"More boxes," said Tobias. "More holes. I'll dig a triple, save work."

Santiago knew he'd never get rid of the bulldog of a marshal. "All right," he said curtly. "Hire a saddle horse and outfit yourself. This'll be an overnight trip. I'll meet you in front of the jail in an hour."

He stalked home dourly and began to check his gear: bedroll, slicker, manacles, ammunition. He threw a box of forty-four caliber brass cartridges into the saddlebag. Plus a bottle of laudanum, some clean bandages and plasters, and a bottle of carbolic.

"Don't go, Santo," said Mimi. "Let him go."

"If he goes alone, there'll be blood spilled," he said, pausing to gather her to him. "Hermes Bragg's dead."

"Oh, Santo. You'd brought him along. I didn't think — "

"It didn't take much, did it. Drag a man four blocks — that's all it took."

"Santo? You're very angry."

"I've never been angrier. Bragg used me for a priest before he died. Shrived himself as best he could. Gave me messages to take to his children and that crew of his — things that could have gotten this mess cleaned up — without Handy."

"Would they believe you?" she asked, her hands tight upon his back.

"I think so, Mimi. They've no reason to doubt me. And good reason to come to Bragg's burial. I'm willing to risk it."

She held him tightly until some of the pressure and rage dissipated. She always did that, healed him, calmed him.

"I'm going, too, Santo!" She broke free and confronted him.

"But Mimi! It's dangerous. You might get shot. You might — "

"Try and stop me. I got a good start talking with Athena Bragg. She trusts me. And don't forget what I carry in my bag."

She always carried a small derringer in her reticule.

He sighed. She would come. She always came if she wished. Her ferocious glare told him she wouldn't be thwarted. This time the need seemed almost volcanic in her. He smiled suddenly. Handy wouldn't like it. But that would be Handy's problem.

Chapter 17

They found Lucullus Handy lounging in front of the sheriff's office and jail, his livery horse tied to the iron ring of one of the six hitching posts there. Santiago knew the liver-colored horse and smiled. Handy would be hard put to keep up, even with a crop. A rolled yellow slicker and blanket curved around the back of the cantle. A double-barreled shotgun with a saddle ring in its butt hung on a leather loop from the saddle horn. Handy had apparently settled for one revolver, which bulged his herringbone suit coat under the left shoulder. On his gray hair perched a black derby that Santiago hadn't seen before.

The federal marshal studied Mimi with agate eyes, noting the full Indian skirts that allowed her to ride astride, her trim calves, and her black hair done in twin braids. Her handbag hung from her saddle horn.

"What's she doing?"

"She's going."

"No she's not."

"She often goes with me."

"You hide behind skirts, do you, Toole?"

Santiago turned hot but chose to ignore it. "She befriended the girl. I think she can persuade Athena to come along."

"She's not going."

"She is and that's all there is to it, Handy."

"It'd be dangerous for her."

"Drovers don't shoot women, Handy."

"I wasn't thinking of that. They could easily snatch her and hold her hostage, and then you'd be dancing to their tune."

"She's going. Now mount up, Handy."

The marshal sighed. "If you insist," he said blandly. He stared at Mimi's red mare. "Ma'am, I hate to be saying it, but your cinch is loose."

"It's tight. And if it isn't, it doesn't matter. I don't ride the way you do."

"It's loose," he said. He stepped toward the horse while she eyed him narrowly, and stuck three fingers under the latigo. "See?" He smiled gently. "Step down and I'll tighten it."

She swung down. Like a feral cat he clamped a hand over her wrist and then a manacle. When that snapped he tugged her hard and snapped the other wrist-ring to the hitching post ring.

"What are you doing?" Santiago roared.

"She stays." Handy trotted over to his horse. "They'll saw the manacle off in an hour. Let's go."

"I'm not going anywhere. Unlock her, Handy!"

257

Lucullus Handy smiled benignly at Santiago. "Come along, Sheriff. Or is it Doctor? I'm plum confused."

"Go ahead."

"Do I have to force you, Doctor?" Handy's eyes mocked.

Santiago boiled. A spectacle in front of the whole of Miles City. Even now pedestrians across Main Street gawked.

Mimi stood beside the hitching post, caught to it by iron. The wild rage in her eyes subsided, and she began to coax her mare to her. She wanted her bag with the revolver in it, Santiago knew. He shook his head at her, but she ignored him. The mare stood, unmoving, reins on the ground.

Handy reached for Santiago's reins, but the sheriff kicked his big bay forward a step or two. "Go ahead, Marshal. I'm staying here to free my wife."

Handy grinned. "That's what I mean."

"Handy, it's a free country. At least until you got off the train."

"I have warrants to serve, Toole. Let's go." Handy untied his livery horse and swung up while wheeling the horse westward. Santiago didn't follow. He swung down from the bay and tied it, then examined the manacle pinning Mimi, wondering if his own keys would work. They wouldn't. Another brand.

"Get me my bag, Santo," she hissed. "He needs some lessons."

"I'd better get the smith," he muttered. Hamlet Dansk could nip the chain in minutes with brawn and a hacksaw. He turned toward east Main only to find Handy back on the ground, grinning, blocking the way.

"You coming or do I drag you — sheriff?"

Santiago raged. A spectacle on Main Street. Holy Mary. He eyed the burly marshal before him, noting slabs of muscle, bull neck, legs that could hold up a piano, fists the size of bowling balls. The marshal had fifty pounds on him and a longer reach.

"You coming, Dr. Toole?" the man asked, smirking.

"Well, me lad, if you put it that way — I'm not."

Handy approached like a grizzly, flat-footed, not bothering to assume any sort of boxing stance.

Santiago slipped out of his black frock coat and undid his black gunbelt and set these items near Mimi.

"Don't!" she hissed. "Give me my bag!"

But Santiago was remembering younger days, back in Kilkenny, pub-crawling days, days filled with ale and laughter, bloody noses, yanked ears, and busted teeth. The blood rose in him, flooding him with energy.

Handy advanced, smirking, a bulldog stalking a terrier.

"Santo . . ." Mimi moaned.

People came close now, exiting mercantiles, clotting into gawking knots.

"Some sheriff," said Handy. "Hides behind skirts."

Santiago let the insult slide by. They circled each other out on the clay street, stepping through clots of manure. Always Handy advanced and Santiago retreated. Handy maneuvered him toward the hitching post and beyond it to the dun stone wall of the sheriff's office.

"A mick. A mick doctor trying to do a man's work."

Mimi spat. It landed on Handy's cheek. He whirled like a lion and yanked one of her braids so hard she toppled to the ground into a pile of manure.

Her horse sidled closer to the hitching post.

He laughed.

Santiago chose the moment. His swift uppercut landed in Handy's iron gut. Santiago's boot swung behind Handy's and toppled the marshal. He sprang up swiftly.

"A spectacle," said Santiago. "You're disturbing the peace. I think I'll have to arrest you."

Handy roared and bulled in, his hams swinging in short, brutal chops that pounded Santiago's arms and shoulders. Every blow sent a numbing shock through Santiago. Even a tap from the massive fists drove deep hurt into him. Santiago dodged and blocked, knowing intuitively what the big man would do. He sliced a fist through Handy's defenses and caught Handy's nose, starting a trickle of bright blood.

"Breaking the peace! Five dollars and expenses!" Pericles Shaw shouted at them and punctuated his shout with two sharp blasts of his revolver. Santiago felt sand sting his legs. Handy laughed and swung hard, the fist slamming through to Santiago's chest; he reeled backward. Handy grinned, licked blood, and bulled forward. His next fist aimed low, for Santiago's groin, but Santiago turned slightly so it landed on the pelvic bone, hurting Handy as much as it hurt Santiago.

Low blows, then. Santiago fought fair as long as his opponent fought fair. He'd learned how to fight the other way, too. He'd met masters in Kilkenny and had taken some bloody lessons.

He kicked a certain spot on the side of Handy's knee, and the marshal gasped. A blow just there, on the side of the knee, hurt more than any other to the human body.

Just for good measure, Santiago kicked at the other knee, a glancing blow that didn't hurt the way his first one did. Handy's face went gray, and he lurched violently on the hurt knee.

"Disturbing the peace," yelled Pericles. "Two lawmen brawling." Another crack, and Santiago felt sand blister his ankles. Pericles Shaw laughed. "Winner takes all," he added.

Santiago circled, fearing the wild, murderous glare in Handy's eyes. The man's crazed look told Santiago that he was out of control and would kill now if he could. He gasped every time he put weight on that knee. Which was fine with Santiago.

The sheriff dropped his hands suddenly, stood stock-still, inviting a lunge. Handy took him up, a wild killer rage radiating hotly from him. He lunged forward, his fists jabbing murderously low, aiming for the groin, aiming to fold Santiago in two and capsize him. But Santiago sidestepped, turned, and caught the side of the knee again, this time with the full force of his boot.

"Arrghah!" gasped Handy, tears rising in his stricken granite face.

"Kill him!" yelled Mimi.

Santiago didn't need to. He swung around and jabbed his boot again into the knee, sending more excruciating pain through

262

Handy. The man screamed, clutched at the knee wildly, and rolled to the clay, gasping. Santiago walked around and booted the other knee. Handy screamed again and writhed on the ground.

He watched, catching his breath, while Handy writhed like a dying snake. "You're under arrest, Handy. Disturbing the peace. Assaulting a peace officer," he rasped between breaths. He found manacles of his own in his saddlebag and snapped them over Handy's thick wrists. They barely encompassed them. Handy lashed out with both hands, sending Santiago flying back. Santiago circled around the seated man and booted the knee again, making the marshal shriek, a wild, eerie, insane howl that sent shivers through Santiago.

"Get up!" he snapped. But Handy sobbed and gasped at the vicious pain rising from his knees.

"Pericles, help me carry this galoot to a cell."

Between them they stood Handy up, wary of the two manacled hands. But pain had taken the brawl out of Handy. Santiago dug in the man's suit coat pocket, found the key to the manacle that trapped Mimi, and unlocked her. Then he picked up Handy's Colt, which had skidded out into the street, and gingerly patted down the marshal, expecting the worst. He confiscated a jackknife.

"Kill him!" Mimi muttered, going for her reticule.

"Don't."

But she didn't listen. She pulled her little five-shot, thirty-two caliber revolver and jabbed it into Handy's back.

"March!" she hissed.

"Watch out, Mimi — he can spin."

She took the warning this time and stood back. Handy stared at her, alarmed, and limped toward the jail.

"Still hiding behind skirts," he muttered.

Santiago booted him on the side of the knee again. Handy screamed and collapsed. The Miles City crowd hooted and cheered. They knew Dr. Toole a lot better than Handy did.

This time Handy didn't resist. Pericles Shaw, the blacksmith Dansk, Santiago, and two merchants hustled Lucullus Handy into the cell next to where Hermes Bragg still lay, and Pericles Shaw locked the clanging door with a satisfying twist of the key.

"Attacking a peace officer, unlawful arrest of Mimi, breaking the peace, and anything else you can think of," Santiago said. His knuckles hurt. He'd skinned them in several places. He hoped it wouldn't interfere with his doctoring.

"Oh, my, Toole, that'll help the coffers. County's plumb broke," said Pericles. "How about fifty on each count?"

Santiago grinned. "I have to get going. Tell Chang Loon we got a prisoner to feed. I'm deputizing you again, Pericles. But don't go near that cell. He'll bust your head in. I've got to go on out to that Bragg outfit and fetch them in."

From within, Handy groaned.

"Leave him manacled. It does something for the soul," Toole directed.

Handy glared. "I'll kill you when I get out, Toole," he muttered. "Where'd you learn about knees? I didn't know about knees."

"A scandal. Federal marshal trying to abduct a sheriff. Ah, yes, abduction. Add that to the list, Pericles."

"Oh, abduction, that's a good one. Worth a hundred, I'd say."

"I'll land the whole federal government on you, Toole," muttered Handy. "Get me Wade at the fort."

"Threatening lawmen," said Pericles. "We all heard it. Custer County's getting plumb rich by the minute."

Santiago grunted. "Pericles, if Handy had won and tossed me in here, you'd probably be fining me."

Shaw surveyed him soberly. "That's right, Sheriff. Disturbing the peace. Resisting arrest. Attacking a federal lawman. Should of brung in two hundred dollars from you, calculating conservatively."

"I knew it. Loyal as a rattler."

Pericles smiled benignly.

"There were lots of witnesses," said Santiago. "And I can't wait here any more. You take statements. And send word out to Adelbert Hoffmeister to attend the Rock girl."

"Oh, count on it, count on it. The more witnesses, the larger the fines," said Pericles.

"Get that corpse outa here," growled Handy.

Hermes Bragg lay in the next cell, small and emaciated. Sylvane Tobias had not come for him.

"He'll stay right there until Sylvane's ready," said Santiago. "In fact, you can think about him. You killed him, dragging him over here."

"When I arrest, I arrest," Handy said. "Cover his face anyway. I don't like those staring eyes."

Bragg's eyes did stare sightlessly at the gloomy plank ceiling twelve feet up. Silently Santiago slipped into the next cell and drew Bragg's blanket over the face, more out of respect for Hermes Bragg than to hide death

266

from Lucullus Handy.

His skinned knuckles hurt. He realized suddenly he'd dragged a blanket laden with consumption bacilli with open wounds on his hands. Muttering, he dug into his Gladstone and wiped them carefully with carbolic. Mimi watched intently.

"Get me a lawyer, Toole. He'll write me a habeas corpus," yelled Handy. "And when I get out, Toole, your knees are going to know it."

"That should net the county another fifty, don't you think, Pericles?"

Suddenly Santiago felt exhausted. Since dawn the day had yielded chaos. Handy's arrival, Bragg's death, this brawl, and all the rest. He nodded to Mimi, and they walked to the door, only to find a crowd there waiting for news.

"He's been arrested. His name's Lucullus Handy, and he's a federal deputy marshal who decided to do things his own way, law or not."

"Can you arrest a marshal?" asked Horton Gatz, the merchant.

"I can arrest anyone who breaks our law. That's all the news I've got."

He swung up into the saddle of his big bay gelding and waited for Mimi. She checked her cinch, found it to be tight, and mounted herself, adjusting her stained skirts, while merchants admired her slim calves.

Santiago steered them west, away from the milling onlookers. Let Pericles handle them, he thought. He slumped in his saddle, trying to recover energy, but the morning had drained everything out of him. He and Mimi walked their mounts westward past saloon row and out beyond town, across the Tongue River bridge, and along the south bank of the aquamarine river.

The day's gloom lifted, and the thin overcast seemed less heavy. Handy had been a dark cloud in his own right. Mimi kicked her mare until it walked beside his gelding, and they forged ahead.

"I'm glad he's in jail," said Mimi. "He killed Hermes Bragg just as if he'd shot him."

"I'll let him cool there a day or two," said Santiago. "I'll have the federal government on my neck, but so what?"

His knuckles still stung, and his shoulders and upper arms ached where they'd taken Handy's terrible hammering. Still, his pain was nothing compared to what probably radiated from Handy's knees.

It'd turned out well, he thought. He and Mimi could deal with the Bragg crew without the menace of that marshal making the Bragg children and the drovers nervous. Still, he sensed that he rode into stark danger, possibly danger that Handy could prevent if he were along, backing things up. For a moment Santiago regretted not having the marshal and then shrugged. What was done was done.

They rode west along the river through a great peace. Ducks and Canada geese clustered in eddies and backwaters, flapping upward and circling around as the horses passed. He planned to ride along the south bank for about ten miles, well west of the fort, to a ford near a colony of Norwegians farming the north bank. Usually the deep, cold river couldn't be forded, but this time of year, at the end of summer and before the fall rains, travelers used a hardbottomed ford that usually wet a horse's belly and threatened to upset the animal. The only other option was to hail the Norwegians and persuade them to ferry Mimi and himself across in a rowboat while the horses swam.

They reached the ford late in the afternoon, in a strange, anemic light somewhere between sun and cloud. Mimi smiled at him. They'd done this before. The river rolled green and chill before them, wider here than elsewhere, and much of it no more than hock-deep. But on the north side there'd be a drop into the main channel, and if they were lucky, they would walk their struggling mounts across fifty yards of swirling water without being upset.

Santiago stepped down and pulled his high-top shoes off and tied the laces. These and his black lisle stockings he slung over his neck. Mimi elected to do nothing: she'd lift her legs or let them soak, Indian-style, and be done with it. He remounted and kicked his reluctant bay into the cold water, which rolled by slowly. He hammered the bay's ribs with his bare heels while it minced gingerly into the current, feeling its way as carefully as a blind man. Behind him he heard Mimi muttering at the mare and the splash of the smaller animal's legs.

Slowly they rode the hard bottom northward. It dropped sickeningly; water swirled around the bay's belly and threatened to capsize the animal, but it found its footing and soon clambered up to shallows and then out upon the north shore. Mimi followed, laughing, more engulfed in cold water on the smaller mare, her skirts soaking up the cold. Then she climbed out. The horses shook violently, spraying cold water.

Santiago put his shoes on, and they rode up the bluffs, past small Scandinavian farms, and out upon the sweeping prairie hills beyond. Within a mile they found the broad swath of trampled grass and manure that marked the passage of a large herd. They turned onto it, wondering where it would lead.

Chapter 18

They rode west, paralleling the distant gray river, down a long swath of trampled coppery grass that ran uphill and down over rugged prairie. At dusk Santiago rode to the top of a long ridge and gazed into the murky pink sunset, finding nothing. He waited quietly, hoping to catch the flare of a distant fire, but none showed itself. The Bragg outfit had made good time, perhaps driving well into the evening.

He nodded to Mimi, and they turned their weary horses into a coulee dotted with cottonwoods with a small spring at its head. It would be their home for the night. A wolf streaked off as they rode roughly downhill. Two crows flapped up. Santiago left the campsites to Mimi because something in her Assiniboin soul knew how to pick the best place to make themselves comfortable. He eyed the sky warily, noting a thin overcast that blurred stars. They lacked a tent, and cold autumnal rain would be miserable.

She picked a spot on a small bench above the dry water-course; a grassy park surrounded by cottonwood and rosy willow brush. They could build a fire here and the hills and brush would hide it from hostile eyes. Swiftly she built a tiny fire, scarcely the width of two hands, and began heating water. Santiago knew it'd be for tea. They traveled light this time, with a long hard loaf of bread, some cheese, and a fat spiced sausage. She had a handful of jerked beef for emergencies and that was it. Except for tea. He'd brought his taste for tea with him from Ireland and simply had to have it or he would turn cantankerous. She'd learned that swiftly and always carried a small tin pot, a cannister of tea, metal cups, and a little strainer.

Night settled and chill air flowed downslope across their flat, driving both the heat and smoke from the tiny fire away from them. Santiago unrolled their sougans, a blanket and canvas tarp, and laid them out windward of the fire. He picketed the horses on coarse grass and for good measure hobbled their forelegs. He'd brought a double-barreled shotgun loaded with buckshot, and this he slid from its saddle sheath and laid beside his bedroll. He watched his gelding crop silently in the dark; then he rubbed it with handfuls of grass, especially where the saddle had slicked down the hair. He rubbed the mare next and returned quietly to the little amber fire, happy to share Mimi's good company

273

and a steaming cup of pungent tea. Lucky in love, he thought. He'd been lucky in love.

They ate and slumped near the fire, feeling the long hours in the saddle on their rumps and inner thighs and knees. It always seemed remarkable to him that cowboys could virtually live in their saddles and rarely know discomfort.

"Santo, what are you going to do?"

She looked across at him in the wavering amber light that made her eyes shine and her flesh dark as walnut. She held her cup in both hands, sipping gingerly.

"I won't know that until I see what kind of reception we get," he said, staring into the fire, knowing it blinded him to do so. In the distant dark he heard the skittering of a small animal. Coulees teemed with life.

"I have a bad feeling about it."

"I do, too. Somehow I've got to get in and talk. I think Jefferson Gonzales will help."

"I think you might get — hurt. No, Santo, hurt isn't the word. I'm afraid for your life."

"A sheriff faces it. A doctor does, too, but from bullets too small to see with the naked eye."

"Let me go in alone, Santo."

"Then they'll have a captive. Make me dance to their tune, as Handy put it."

"But we'll both be alive at the end."

Santiago peered down at the steel star on his black vest, glinting yellow in the dancing light. "This says something to them. It means the same thing in Montana that it does in Texas."

Mimi snorted. "Some of them won't care. Some will think it's a target."

Santiago fed dry sticks into the little fire, squaw wood Mimi had broken off the underside of trees. A faint new warmth radiated outward, heating the black wool of his vest even while his backside felt chill in the downdraft.

"Maybe it'll be a target, Mimi. Could you bear it?"

"You dying?"

"Yes. Me dying."

"Oh, Santo. We need a posse."

"I'm doing it this way for three people; Apollo first; Jefferson Gonzales second; and Athena, though I don't know that I can bring her around. And for a fourth — Hermes Bragg. He entrusted me with this task."

"Hold me," she said.

He slid over to her sougan and pulled her close to him, feeling her young cheek on his, the slimness of her long body, and the beat of her heart. She felt good in his arms, and as he pressed her, she settled gently into him.

"Oh, Santo," she whispered in his ear. "I've never been so afraid."

"I'm not very brave," he admitted. He ran his hand down her spine, pausing at each familiar bump. He wondered if he'd desire her soon. Not now. For the moment they comforted each other against the dread of the morrow. He heard something move softly in the brush and stared out past her jet hair pressing his face to see what he could. Nothing.

"If something happens to me, go back for help fast. Maybe even release Handy."

He knew she wouldn't. If something happened to him, she'd flee directly north to the band of her mother, high up on the Milk River, above the Missouri. In Miles City he was her bulwark and safety among whites who had no use for people of other blood. Like Sylvane Tobias, he thought wearily. A good man but one with pronounced opinions about Indians, Mexicans, and anyone else he chose to scorn.

He held her for a long time, the better part of an hour, feeling her relax in his arms and then grow heavy as sleep overtook her. He held her until his muscles hurt and he wanted to let go; but still he held her. It might be the last time he held her. He hoped not. He had no intention of dying and no intention of being a foolish hero, one against many. Still, tomorrow he'd face nervous men with guns, men he could accuse of several crimes. And any one of them might do the blind, violent thing he dreaded.

Quietly he settled her in her bedroll, pausing to admire her in the ember-glow. The last orange caught the sharp, clean lines of her face and glinted from her loose, long black hair that swirled over her slim breast.

"I love you, Mimi," he said aloud, and tucked the blanket and its canvas cover about her. Her hand caught his and held it.

He stood in the night, his eyes keen now that the fire had died. He stood listening, absorbing the rhythms of this place. He'd learned these things from Mimi; learned to attune himself to nature and come awake when something changed, some rhythm broke. He picked up the shotgun and walked quietly upslope through bunchgrass to the west ridge and stood there, stopping wind that eddied icily into his frock coat and over his face. No stars in the great impenetrable blackness. And yet — off some vast distance he spotted the thing he'd missed earlier, a prick of light in the young evening. Farther north than he had looked before. They were leaving the Yellowstone, then, following some creek northwest. He couldn't imagine how far that wavering bit of light was from him. Several miles, he imagined. He and Mimi would catch up in the morning probably.

He thought briefly of saddling up right then and riding toward that light. He had a simple message for the Bragg children: Hermes had died. After that, he thought he could persuade them to return. Especially when they learned that he'd dealt with Handy. But it was daytime work, not something for the stealth of night.

The shot split the peace into bits. It cracked out of the blackness, raping the silence. It sent a pulse of terror through Santiago that started his heart slamming. He had no idea whether the bullet had come close, but he didn't wait to find out. He dove to earth, glancing back fearfully at the still figure close to the coals behind him.

"Toole! I know you're there."

Santiago remained silent.

"Toole. You think we don't know you're following us? What do you take us for? We're the Bragg outfit. Go back. Go back or die. Forget us. We're on our way."

Santiago tried to place the voice but couldn't. It had a Texas slur to it, and it could have been any one of them. He debated answering and decided to find some crease in the land first. He slid left, downslope slightly, wishing the embers behind him were out, embers that still revealed Mimi's sleeping form.

"Who's calling?" Santiago yelled, and ducked instantly, pressing his head to the cold clay.

He heard only laughter.

He debated trying again. His black suit helped, he knew. "I have news. Are you listening?"

He heard nothing.

"Hermes Bragg is dead. He left messages for his children."

"Nice try, Toole." The voice didn't seem far away at all.

"I'm coming in tomorrow. I promised Hermes Bragg I would."

The response was a shot, violent in the night, that blew the embers of the dying fire in all directions. The flash had come from just up the ridge. Below, he glimpsed Mimi crawling toward darkness. Above he heard laughter and then nothing at all.

Neither of them slept. By gray dawn they were stiff, cold, and bone-tired. And sullen. Who could sleep when men with guns prowled? Who could drive darkness from his mind when death loomed with every whisper of the brush? He stared at Mimi in the cold pewter light and saw deep circles under her eyes, weariness there to match his own.

She rose tiredly and started one of her tiny fires to make tea. By unspoken agreement they'd have only tea this morning. Their stomachs wouldn't tolerate more. He sat stiffly, rubbing a hand across his stubbled face. He always felt naked without a shave. His Nero strop and Durham straightedge had become a morning ritual for him, as important to his sense of well-being as morning coffee was to many. Mimi hadn't understood that at first: her French father had a great black beard, and her mother's Assiniboin people lacked facial hair. At first she'd stared at him each morning when he began his ritual, watching him lather with his brush and then scrape away beard the way her mother scraped buffalo hide.

She handed him tea, the other half of his morning ritual. She drank it, too; it had become as narcotic for her as it was for him. The acrid steam at his nostrils was the only thing to make this forbidding dawn bearable.

"Do you want to go back?" he asked.

She shook her head.

"I do. But I won't. Cowards die a thousand times before their deaths, but the valiant die only once. Shakespeare said that and he was right — even if he was a damned Englishman. And I know what I am."

"On, Santo." She grinned.

He laughed, too, thinly. Death was a part of both his professions, and he never escaped it long. Religion helped a little, but not much. He didn't want to die. Not so young, not with Mimi, in all her glory, sharing life with him.

"It's a good day to die," she said.

He sucked the last of the Earl Grey tea and shook bitter dregs to the ground. It hadn't comforted and calmed him the way it usually did.

In minutes they broke camp, saddled, and rode off into the dark and sunless west, topping each long ridge cautiously. When the light thickened, distant things leapt close. From the next ridge he spotted the herd, a long sinuous snake of dark cattle coiling up the valley of a slim silvery creek under a tin sky. It made his stomach lurch.

They gained ground swiftly. Their horses weren't tired, even if the riders were, and both animals jogged eagerly into the eddying cool air. He felt the powerful limbs of the thoroughbred under him and its strange heat, the heat of a breed trained to race. This one he'd purchased from Marcus Daly, the silver king over in Butte who loved Irish horseflesh as much as Santiago did. An extravagance. Three hundred dollars. Almost as much as Santiago cleared in a year from the practice of country medicine.

Riding at a steady jog, they gained about two miles an hour on the distant herd. From ridge tops now they could see individual animals, dark dots crawling along with innumerable other dark dots heading west by northwest. Mimi rode grimly beside him, her eyes alert, seeing things white men didn't see. He felt a tightness across his chest and knew it to be tension, the kind of taut contraction of muscle that wearied a man faster than hard labor. He searched for the wagons from one rise, wanting to know where in that long snake the children were. Not at drag, with wind whipping dust of over two thousand beeves at them. He spotted them at last on the western flank, to the left of the herd, about at the middle.

In another hour their jogging brought them close to the drag riders, half a dozen of them, wearing bandannas over their faces to keep the whipping grit out of their nostrils. The drag riders in turn saw Santiago and Mimi coming and kept looking behind them. Then the herd rounded a vast low shoulder of grassy hills and disappeared, while Santiago and Mimi rode across a low basin full of wallows where buffalo had lingered only a year or two before.

When they topped the far western shoulder of the basin, Santiago saw at once it was too late. Before them, fifty yards off, stood a line of drag riders, bandannas up, carbines in hand, waiting. A harsh wind whipped the tails and manes of their ponies and flapped their collars. All six of the drag riders held glinting Winchesters across their laps.

Santiago pulled his reins lightly, and the bay stopped.

"I have a message for the Braggs," he shouted.

"Go away, Toole," yelled one of the cowboys.

"A message from Hermes Bragg," Santiago yelled back. His voice had gone hoarse with tiredness and tension.

"Turn back or die."

"Santo — don't."

"I'm taking my message. To the wagons." Santiago shouted it back at them and turned the big bay left, intending to go around and up the left flank.

A shot racketed through the whipping air, and dust puffed in front of the bay.

Santiago paused, reached into his saddlebag, and dug around for a sheet of white cotton bandaging he kept there. He found it and tied it to the barrel of his shotgun and raised it. They'd respect a white flag.

The drag riders watched motionlessly, wind whipping through them. Santiago raised his shotgun with its truce flag and kicked his bay in the ribs.

All six of the drag riders lifted their carbines in a single fluid motion and shot. Santiago felt the thump of lead striking his big bay. The animal halted, quivered, coughed, braced itself on four legs, dropped its head, and then began quaking. Santiago sat stunned and then leapt off, using the collapsing horse for cover.

Mimi yelled and kicked her pony over to him.

The great bay, gouting blood from its mouth and nose, sighed, shook, and collapsed.

"You heard us, Toole. We meant it," yelled the drag rider who'd done the shouting.

"Holy Mary," he cried. The horse pawed earth, trembled, and died.

He heard laughter, and then the six cowboys wheeled their ponies and trotted off to hurry the laggards along. In moments, they disappeared around the bend, and only the whipping wind remained. The horse leaked a little blood, and then the flow stopped.

"Holy Mary," he muttered again, unable to think.

Mimi dismounted and began tugging at the latigo to release the cinch on the dead horse.

"Help me, Santo."

But he couldn't. He stared paralyzed at the horse, at her tugging hard at the pinned saddle, at the blood sinking into dun clay. Then he collected his wits and helped her. It took both of them to yank the pinned fender and stirrup free. His hands trembled.

Feeling stupid, he untied his white flag and folded the cotton and returned it to his saddlebag. He worked numbly, knowing that his Irish was up, and he'd be so mad he would be out of control. His great bay horse murdered. He stared at the manure-laden swath of broken grass and hated them all, loathed those Braggs with a searing hot fire that would flare in him until he'd finished this job.

"Santo — "

"I'll walk," he muttered. "Your mare's too small for the two of us. I'll have to get a posse."

"That's not it, Santo. Someone's coming."

She pointed toward the southeast where a lone horseman jogged steadily westward, following the great swath of trampled grasses. They watched him coming, curious at first, and then alarmed. At about two hundred yards distance, the man assumed a familiar

285

shape and so did the horse. The brown horse had been rented at the livery. The blocky man riding it wore gray herringbone and had the look of granite.

Mimi watched narrowly and headed for her bag. Santiago didn't stop her.

Handy rode up, surveyed the wreckage with glinting black eyes that flashed mocking messages, and smiled.

"You needed me, Toole."

"How'd you get out?"

Handy chuckled. "Never make deputies out of old justices, Toole. I lured old Pericles to the cell, and when he got close I grabbed him. Amazing how easy it is to choke a man who's on the other side of bars."

A cold dread swept through Santiago. "You killed him — "

"Naw. I got an arm around his throat, dug in his pocket for the keys, tossed him down, and unlocked myself. You got some jail, Toole."

Handy sat his saddle, mocking.

"Get off that horse, Marshal." Mimi's sharp voice pierced through the wind. She gripped her five-shot, thirty-two revolver in her hand and aimed it squarely at the marshal's heart.

He stared, surprised. "You wouldn't," he said.

She shot.

286

Chapter 19

Lucullus Handy's black bowler sailed upward, caught wind, and glided thirty yards, landing at last upside down in sagebrush.

Mimi lowered the shining black revolver again, this time aiming between Handy's eyes. He stared at her, the black agates in his head shrinking to pinheads and burning like phosphorus.

"You're under arrest, madam," he said quietly.

"That's a good one, Handy. You just broke jail." Santiago's Irish had started to consume him, running hot through his chest and arms until he was spoiling for a brawl.

Handy peered at Santiago, faint astonishment in his gaze.

"You're dead, Handy," Santiago added, his voice harsh and tired.

"Local charges. Federal marshals face it all the time. Namby pamby sheriff — or crooked. The Justice Department will deal with it — and you."

Mimi squeezed. The little revolver spat. Something sizzled across Handy's herringbone suit coat. His eyes flared and shrank.

"Put your hands on the saddle horn," she said.

He obeyed methodically.

"Would you mind getting my hat? If you've ruint it, I'll demand the price."

A cool one, Santiago thought. It didn't matter. He was itching to pull the square block of granite off his rental nag and teach him a few more things.

He drew his own Remington and pointed it steadily at the marshal. "Get down, and make it slow and keep your hands visible."

Handy seemed puzzled.

"I'm taking your livery nag. You get to walk."

Handy nodded and did as he was instructed, blinking methodically.

"We might work together," he said at last. "I'll drop charges against your little squaw here if you drop charges."

"Tough luck, Handy."

Bitterness boiled through Santiago. He'd had enough. Had enough of the Braggs and their lawlessness; had enough of this bull-headed marshal. He watched Handy measure him and slowly surrender.

"Braggs got to you, did they?" Handy asked, grinning slightly. "Shooting that blood horse did it."

A good lawman, Santiago admitted. Handy

knew men and knew a rage when he saw it. "Back away from that nag and keep your hands up," Santiago whispered.

Handy nodded warily and did so.

Santiago wondered what to do next. Handy had a weapon in a shoulder rig. He decided to ignore it.

"Put your arms behind your back," he said. "Mimi, keep an eye on him. I'm going to lock him. I don't take jailbreak kindly."

She nodded and kicked her mare closer, her little black revolver never wavering.

"Lie down on your stomach. If I see a hand move toward that shoulder gun, I'll shoot."

Something in Santiago's biting tone won Handy's respect. Slowly he settled to his knees and then down on his belly, hands carefully away from his torso.

Santiago dug his manacles from his saddlebag and snapped them over Handy's wrists.

"Roll over."

Handy did, and Santiago plucked out the revolver nestled under Handy's left armpit. With a wave of it, he motioned Handy to sit up.

"All right. Walk back to Miles."

Lucullus Handy's face sagged. Santiago knew why. It was twice as hard to walk with arms locked behind than when the arms were free and swinging as counterweights to the movement of the legs.

"I'll make a deal," Handy said.

"No deals. I'm tired of you. You've busted laws. You've wrecked my plans. You've said I'm crooked. I'm interested in justice, not just throwing convenient bodies in jail."

"That's what I'm talking about."

"No deals."

Handy stared sourly. Santiago saw rage in him.

"You'll learn what happens to punks that mess with United States marshals."

"Santo — "

Mimi pointed north. On the crest of a hill two distant horsemen stood. She slid her revolver into her reticule. That's how she always played it: ace in the hole. The riders spurred their animals and rode in slowly, while Santiago watched dourly, ready for anything. Handy looked puzzled.

"We're coming in, Toole."

Santiago thought he recognized the distant voice, but he wasn't sure. He thought he recognized the riders, too. They approached carefully, hands on reins. Drovers, both of them, wide-brimmed hats, red bandannas, chaps. He watched their ponies pick their way down a gentle slope into the basin. Jefferson Gonzales and Apollo. They stopped ten yards off, taking in Handy sitting on the dun earth, hands clamped behind him, and then the humped sprawl of the dead thoroughbred. Santiago waited, still full of cold rage.

"We slipped out. Through the dust on the downwind side and around a coulee," said Gonzales tentatively. "They passed word up the line. You said Hermes is dead, and you have messages."

Santiago nodded curtly.

The segundo's bright blue eyes steadied on the dead horse. "I didn't know about that," he said quietly. "That's a terrible thing, horseflesh like that."

Santiago stared.

"The boy's sick. He took a fever after swimming the river again. I brought him to you."

Santiago spotted the fever in Apollo's face and the lad's misery. "Apollo, get down and wrap up in a sougan over there. I'll get to you directly."

The boy slid off his pony.

"Sheriff — we're here to help. We've been prisoners, at least until we saw our chance."

Santiago met the gaze of those blue eyes and nodded. "Hermes died yesterday morning. After that marshal there dragged him four blocks to my jail against my wishes. He had a federal warrant, and I couldn't stop him. Not even as a doctor. I'm going to charge him with manslaughter for it."

Handy stared at one and another of them, unblinking.

"Yesterday I locked him up for breaking several laws. Then he busted out. Just in case you're wondering."

"Can you do that — arrest a federal marshal?"

"I can arrest anyone who breaks the laws I enforce."

Gonzales nodded.

"Handy there has a federal warrant for everyone in the Bragg outfit," Santiago added malevolently.

"I knew it'd come to that," Gonzales said. "It's worse now, Sheriff. That girl's gone plumb outlaw. At age fifteen. Today's her birthday. At fifteen she's taken over, and she's got six or eight others with her, making it stick. She's gotten plumb twisted, Sheriff. She doesn't care if her old man's gone. Or if he left her a message. She's gone mean, like her pa raised her."

Santiago sighed. "That's the message he left, Gonzales. I don't know whether he was looking ahead and deciding to hedge his bets about an afterlife or whether he just wanted to die right. He wanted me to tell Athena and Apollo he'd been wrong. To bring the herd back and cut out the stolen beeves. He tried to say he loved them but couldn't quite manage that. But he said it anyway, with the trying."

Tears slid down Apollo's fevered face. The boy sat nearby with a blanket drawn around him.

"He wanted you all to come to his burying."

Gonzales stared off into the thin overcast. "The boy and I'll come. And then we'll face your music."

"Gonzales, I don't see that either of you face any charges. You fought Bragg every step of the way and tried to stop it. Apollo here wasn't involved in it and lived in fear of his father."

"Federal charges," said Gonzales.

Santiago nodded. "I think the marshal here is listening."

The segundo squinted at the west horizon. "I think they'll come after us soon. They've found out we're missing by now."

"Gonzales, I need a list fast. Two lists. First, which of those cowboys are in with the girl and enforcing her orders?"

"Corkscrew is her segundo, crowding me out. Snakehead, the cavvy wrangler. Plutarch Gantt, Jasper Higgins, Sugarmouth — that's Wilbur Scruggs, Constable Reilly — "

"Constable?"

"That's his handle. Constable. Connie. Couple more I'm not sure of."

Santiago nodded. "They've got the rest buffaloed?"

"They're all handy with six-guns and ready to use them. Too ready."

"Gonzales — if you can do it — would you tell me who helped Bragg? Who I should charge and who I should let go?"

The segundo grinned. "Same bunch. After the herd sucked in the Indian beeves, the rest of us tried to cut them out — and that bunch stopped us. When the fight came that bunch hung around the Bragg wagon and got into it. The rest were back on flank or drag. Except me. I was there at the fight, Toole."

"You shoot?"

"I had my carbine out. I didn't want them killing Hermes or Apollo or Miss Athena."

"Those hardcases. They're coming after you now? Any others?"

"Most of the others are ciphers, Toole. They take orders and keep their mouths shut. Except the cookie. He's raring to stomp them."

"His name?"

"Purgatory."

"What's that stand for?"

"His chow. Tastes like Purgatory."

"Is he a big black-haired giant with wide shoulders?"

"That's him. He hated the whole crooked business from the beginning and didn't mind saying it. I hope he survives."

From the ground, Handy spoke up. "Gonzales, is that the list I should nip?"

Gonzales replied blandly. "When you get out of jail, I'd say that's the list. Two fence-sitters I'm not sure about. Miss Athena, I don't know. She's just a girl."

"She went bad," said Apollo.

Handy stood awkwardly. "Let me go, Toole, and those are the ones I'll nip."

"I don't deal," snapped Santiago, hotter than ever.

Handy's black agates followed him, unblinking.

"Watch for trouble. I'll see to this boy," Santiago said, digging into his saddlebag for a stethoscope. He lacked a thermometer, but the boy was plainly flushed and feverish, his extremities icy. He'd heard the boy cough while they talked.

"You coughing a lot, lad?"

Apollo nodded.

"Let's see your throat."

Sore. Not as bad as some. He pressed his stethoscope to the boy's chest, listening carefully. The young heart beat rapidly but seemed strong and pumped steadily. He heard the congestion in the right lung: fluids, pneumonia. The left seemed better, clear at the bottom — but not above. He listened closely, jabbing the instrument around and about, jabbing and listening. A familiar rumble and gurgle. He listened again, hating it, hating this. Six months or so in that wagon with his father had done it. He pressed the boy's lymph glands, finding them swollen and lumpy. It often wrecked the lymph system as fast as it demolished lungs. He stood somberly, staring out at nothing, full of emptiness. Apollo would be dead within a year if he survived the pneumonia.

"You've got pneumonia in your right lung," he said. "We've got to get you to bed fast, lad."

He didn't say the rest.

"Santo — "

He peered up at Mimi and followed her gaze. Seven horsemen on a distant western ridge. They reined in for a minute, studying what lay below, and then broke into two columns, heading around each flank.

"Is that them, Gonzales?"

The segundo nodded.

"Better give me my revolver, Toole," said Handy. "So I can defend myself — and you."

"I don't deal."

Handy went white. "You're murdering me."

"It might be negligent manslaughter, Marshal Handy."

The horsemen rode easily now, circling around, cutting off escape. No retreat. It said something about their intentions. The girl was among them, riding in a slit leather skirt. A Bragg indeed.

Santiago watched the distant horsemen, trying to read intent. They were cutting off escape to Miles City, but no one blocked the way toward the herd to the west. Killed or captured, then. But quite possibly there were friends to the west, led by that cook.

"How do you read it, Mr. Gonzales?"

"That's Corkscrew there, and he's fixing to satisfy his itch."

Santiago nodded, wondering how he could avoid that thing. Probably he couldn't. "You know them better than I do. What do they mean to do?"

"Take Apollo, shoot me, kill you and Handy."

"My wife?"

"They don't shoot women. It runs against the soul of a drover. But Corkscrew's no drover."

Santiago picked up his shotgun, wondering not only what they would do but what he wanted to do. He glanced unhappily at Mimi, who sat on her mare with her little revolver in hand but buried in her skirts.

"Jesus, Toole," said Handy. His face sweated now.

"You killed the girl's father."

Handy stared bleakly and walked to the dead horse, lying down behind it.

Apollo squirmed under his blanket and then wrapped it tight around him again.

No chance of forting up, Santiago thought. A flat grassy basin in every direction without a crease in sight. It wouldn't work anyway. Corkscrew's men had carbines and revolvers. Here there were only revolvers and a shotgun. They'd all be shot to bits. No chance of running either — unless they left Handy behind and headed due west, toward the herd. Leave Handy to die. Something in him bridled at that. He didn't want to run. His Irish ran hot in him now, and he'd see this thing through. He'd surprise a few of those Texans.

"I'll deal with them," he said hotly.

Gonzales stared skeptically, revolver in hand. Mimi looked frightened and grim. Apollo sat huddled and feverish under the blanket.

Probably death, Santiago thought. Here he would end. He muttered to himself, driving back fear. He knew he was no hero, knew his rage might doom them all, but the heat boiled through him, and he didn't care. Didn't care that he was a doctor of medicine. Didn't care that he was young and had years left. His pulse climbed, and when Corkscrew indolently turned his pony inward and rode smirking toward the surrounded party, Santiago knew exactly what would come of it. He'd die in a few seconds but not alone.

"I'm telling you, Toole, give me a gun. Unlock me. I'll make the difference."

"My fight."

"Jesus."

The girl turned her pinto inward, too, and rode beside Corkscrew. She had her own carbine across her lap. Even from a distance, she looked full-grown and willful, a woman with designs. Santiago knew at a glance the die had been cast; she'd been molded by Hermes Bragg and would never change.

The loop of surrounding riders tightened, and Santiago's circle grew smaller and smaller. All the horsemen had carbines in their laps, ready for instant use. They stopped at last just beyond shotgun range, safe from everything except a lucky revolver shot. But the girl and her new segundo, Corkscrew, came in grinning. How hard she looked, Santiago thought. Was it the day or two in his jail, or was it something that had been hammered into her for years?

At twenty yards Athena and Corkscrew reined up and surveyed everything. Santiago swung the shotgun tucked in his arm toward Corkscrew but didn't lift it. Corkscrew smirked and let his free hand dangle inches from his holstered revolver. Athena studied old Jefferson Gonzales solemnly, her gray eyes revealing not the slightest emotion. Then she studied Apollo, sick and huddled in a blanket. Then her gaze settled on Mimi, slid away to Santiago, and ended at last upon the prone, gray form of Handy, playing dead behind the horse.

Seconds ticked. No one spoke. Nothing happened. Athena's eyes seemed to focus at last on Santiago's steel star, gleaming on his black waistcoat. Santiago decided to wait them out. He'd done that before, and sometimes the results surprised him. Once, at the end of a taut silence, a small-time hooligan had simply dropped his drawn weapon and sighed. Santiago felt the tension cramping his muscles but held himself quiet, ready for whatever came. He dared not glance away or give Corkscrew any advantage, but he knew he and Mimi and the rest were within easy carbine range from the others.

Something agitated the girl; he could see that. The muscles of her young face spasmed and her chin lifted. A moment later he understood. She lifted her small carbine and shot Jefferson Gonzales in the chest. Wind whipped away the blast. Gonzales flew backward and then righted himself in the saddle. His chest bloomed red. Santiago stared, stunned.

"Miss Athena," whispered Gonzales, "what — "

His bright azure eyes dimmed then, and he began folding up, surrendering piece by piece.

"No one betrays a Bragg."

Jefferson Gonzales capsized and fell over the side, hitting the clay with his head and shoulders while his boot and spur hung in the stirrup.

"Athena!" cried Apollo.

She levered her carbine and swung it toward her brother. Mimi shot from the right. The back of Athena's hand bloomed red, and the carbine careened to the ground. She shrieked, an eerie howl like a bitch wolf dying, and jammed the pulp of her hand into her stomach, bloodying her brown skirts. Corkscrew gaped at Athena, who sat sobbing in her saddle, and then swung back to Santiago. Too late. A load of double-aught buckshot punched through his chest and neck, and he flew backward off his pony.

From out among the distant riders, carbines

cracked. Other horsemen boiled over a crest. One of them looked like the cook. Santiago dove to earth. He glared around wildly. Off somewhere east he heard the crackle of a fight. He sat up slowly. On the other side of the dead horse, Handy sat grinning. Athena Bragg humped over her gouting hand, screaming weird things that ended in choked sobs. One of her fingers lay in the grass, pink and red. A magpie snatched it and flew off. Jefferson Gonzales's wiry pony side-stepped slowly, trying to edge from the body with one leg caught in a stirrup. The old segundo's head caught in the grass as the horse pulled the body. Jefferson Gonzales had become the color of the earth except for the red on his chest and the trickle of bright blood from his mouth. Corkscrew's pony bucked violently and snapped its teeth at the red smear across its stifle. Corkscrew sprawled on his back, smirking and admiring the pale sun. A ball had knocked out some of his incisors. Mimi sat her horse sternly, watching distant horsemen. She glanced at the girl now and then, without a shred of remorse in her dark eyes.

Apollo sobbed and pressed his eyes shut and coughed.

Santiago stood slowly, trembling, and stumbled toward the screeching girl.

Chapter 20

Nothing like this had ever happened before. And it likely would never happen again. Santiago dreaded it worse than he'd ever dreaded anything in his life. Worse even than when he faced his first cadaver in the bitter-smelling dissecting room at the rear of the teaching hospital in Scotland. He'd thought of resigning, leaving this awful burden to the next man. But he knew he couldn't. This came with the job, and he'd accepted the job years before knowing that it did. But never had any doctor, from the beginning of medicine, ever felt more out of place.

There'd been protests, of course, and uproars back east, and editorials in the *New York Times* and the *New York Herald*. But a sober Miles City jury of good men and true had declared it, and Pericles T. Shaw had pronounced it. And no pardon or clemency had winged its way over wires from Helena — or Washington, D.C. On this appointed December day, Santiago would do what he had to do; what his office required him to do. He had a little room to maneuver, though, and set the event for dawn, hoping to keep the crowds away, hoping the arctic cold and

303

darkness of the north would clamp people indoors. It had been a foolish hope.

He peered out the new-barred window of the sheriff's office and jail, into the dusk of a new day and knew the whole of Miles City would watch. Not just Miles. Reporters had caught the trains, arriving on the Northern Pacific for days, checking into the Commercial Hotel until no rooms remained. Outside Sylvane Tobias's handiwork rose upward. Two posts wide apart and a long heavy crossbar, all above a long platform — long enough to hold four persons, all condemned by the jury to hang by their necks until dead. One of those four was a girl, barely fifteen; an orphan, they said, with a half-healed, shot-up hand. Unheard of. Hanging a girl. How they raged back east. That's what had brought the reporters.

The others were three Texas cowboys whose only crime had been to swipe a few reservation cattle and shoot a couple of Sioux later. That was unheard of, too. Hanging three good Texas cowboys just because they'd killed two redskins. It didn't make sense to most people. They'd done the world a favor actually. It had happened in Santiago's county — this murder of Sioux retrieving their stolen stock — and so it had come to Santiago to do what he had to do, to fulfill the laws laid down by his peers.

He stood at his window watching the silent crowd collect in the gray light, seeing their cold breath. A whole company of soldiers from the fort in heavy buffalo coats patrolled with bayonetted rifles at the ready. Word had filtered in that some considered hanging a fifteen-year-old girl so unspeakable that there'd be a jailbreak.

He had half-a-dozen temporary deputies now, as well as the army, and all of these waited in the tensioned office for the appointed hour of eight — dawn in that solstice season and latitude. Outside he saw several reporters talking shop with each other, their breath steaming. They had arrived scandalized and ready to destroy Santiago and Miles City and Montana Territory with acid pens. But Santiago had taken them one by one to interview the girl, listen to her gloat and boast of murder and theft and being a Bragg, and the reporters had walked away subdued and thoughtful. He tried to hide Apollo from them, but they'd found the boy in Santiago's own home, coughing on a cot in a small ell of the cottage. They had barged in with scarcely a nod to Mimi, who tried to shoo them out. Santiago finally threatened to arrest anyone who trespassed on his property, and that held them off.

Santiago had bound the hand of the screaming girl after amputating another finger that had been pulverized beyond repair. Months later he could still remember her eerie screams rending the quiet basin, hear her awesome curses and contempt and threats and self-pity, all rolled into hysterical raging. Hermes Bragg had twisted her into a monster. Apollo had clapped his hands to his ears and wept and shook his head.

The big dark cook, the one the outfit called Purgatory, had organized his own party of men who'd come to the end of the line with the Braggs, a dozen of them, and had descended on the hardcases, shot three and captured three. Even while Santiago had worked on Athena's hand angrily, for it was a hand that had done murder moments before, Purgatory had ridden in with the three living hardcases. Then, seeing Jefferson Gonzales dead on the naked earth, the cook had sobbed. They'd buried Corkscrew and the other hardcases right there in lonely unmarked holes, well forgotten. But Gonzales they'd wrapped tenderly and brought in to Sylvane Tobias.

By the end of that terrible day the herd had been penned in the corrals beside the Northern Pacific tracks, the Sioux cattle cut out, and the prisoners, including Deputy U.S.

Marshal Lucullus Handy, arraigned on various charges before Pericles Shaw. It had been night then, and Shaw's lantern-lit glare at Handy had been so palpable that it lingered in Santiago's mind. Moments after that he learned that Agate Rock had died at noon.

Santiago sighed unhappily and peered out the dirty window at the dark crowd. A doomsday gray lit the southeastern horizon, bringing tension to his chest. A burly master sergeant from Fort Keogh, DeSoto Graves, had volunteered to do the honors. He'd hanged thirty-seven rebs and deserters in the late conflict and knew the art and craft of nooses and neck-snapping. Santiago felt a flood of relief — and then turned the sergeant down. A man had to do what he had to do. In a few minutes now he'd do what he had to do.

The trial had triggered uproars across the territory. Pericles Shaw had presided, sitting toadlike above them all, pounding the bench with the butt of his empty revolver. At that time of year there was a want of flies. Athena had sold her herd and devoted the whole of it to her defense. She had imported a fancy, muttonchopped Helena lawyer, Cornelius Price Briggander, but not all his flowery rhetoric about orphan girls could save her. Athena didn't testify, but her loud remarks doomed her in the end. It was not just the premeditated murder of Jefferson Gonzales, the old family retainer, that swayed the jury. They learned as well that she had fired earlier at the sheriff, barely missing him, and was taking aim at her own brother the moment Mimi shot her hand. All that plus jailbreak, resisting arrest, and assorted other charges.

From her defendant's seat she had shouted, "When a horse breaks a leg, shoot it." It wasn't in the testimony, but the jury no doubt weighed it. The jury had solemnly debated eleven minutes. They condemned her to hang by the neck until dead, and that had been the beginning of the uproars.

Lucullus Handy had fared slightly better. Two days after Handy's jailbreak Santiago marched him into Shaw's courtroom. The magistrate eyed the marshal malevolently, while Handy returned a sulphurous glare.

"I am a prejudiced judge," Pericles began snappishly. "I've found you guilty before the trial begins. I've testified to myself that you choked me nigh to the grave and dug into my pockets and extracted a brass key to escape lawful incarceration, and after hearing my testimony, I have found you two hundred proof guilty."

He had lifted his battered six-gun and poked it into Handy's face. Handy blinked.

"You can request a new magistrate from Helena, in which case I will delay and make sure you sit in that cold cell a month or three. You can raise a howl and embarrass the Justice Department and the U.S. Marshal Service. I will embarrass them and you by talking to the press and conducting myself in a manner calculated to be not at all judicial. Or you can pay a five-hundred-dollar fine and catch the next train west and never show your ugly mug in Miles City ever more, upon pain of arrest."

Lucullus Handy had blinked and grinned.

He lacked the amount. Three days and several wires to relatives later he had the amount, and Santiago freed him.

"I'll remember you, Toole," was all Handy said as Santiago escorted him to the train station. Santiago guarded his knees.

Santiago never heard any more about the federal warrants. Bragg's drovers had driven the stolen beeves back down to Pine Ridge, and that had been the end of that. Athena had never paid them.

Three minutes to eight. Time to fetch Athena. He rose heavily and sat again, unable to make himself enter the cellroom. Some sheriff, he thought. Outside bundled citizens stood in dirty snow. He momentarily hated them all, hated them for coming to gawk at death, hear necks snap, see bodies twitch and spasm, see eternal darkness settle. At least Mimi wouldn't be there. She was at home, beside the boy. Apollo wouldn't be there either, thank heaven. He'd taken the news that Athena would be hanged solemnly, barely blinking an eye. But later he'd cried, and both Santiago and Mimi had sat beside him, holding him. For days he'd cried about Athena, and then one day he'd stopped crying.

He'd recovered slowly from pneumonia only to lose ground to miliary consumption, the kind that tread over a body with jackboots. It would kill the boy by spring unless some sort of remission occurred, which sometimes happened. The lad had nothing; Santiago cared for him out of charity — and love.

That was Hermes Bragg's legacy: a daughter about to be hanged and a boy who had found his soul but was losing his life. There'd been no one to bury Hermes Bragg when they all returned to Miles City. Apollo had been gravely ill and feverish; Athena refused when Santiago offered to free her long enough for the burial. "He broke a leg," she had shouted.

It had turned into a double burial. Tobias's diggers had prepared a hole over in the Mexican section of the graveyard — again against

Santiago's protests — for Jefferson Gonzales. Three attended: Santiago, Mimi, and the big cook, Purgatory, who wept for both men. It was a sunny day with puffball clouds. They walked slowly behind Tobias's wagon with its burden of boxes, walked wearily up the long dry grade to the windswept prairie meadow on top, on a sunny day with puffball clouds, and buried two men.

No one had said much of anything. They stood with hats off, bowed before their maker. Then Purgatory, looking uncomfortable in new store-bought britches and boots, took it upon himself to say something over Hermes Bragg.

"I worked for a good man," he said firmly. "Until close to the end of his days, he was a man to settle the West and tame the wild lands. He talked hard and acted gentle, for the most part. Until the last two or three years, anyway. He had a dark streak, and may God forgive it. A streak that hurt his children and destroyed a marriage. But Hermes Bragg was a man. A man, I say."

Amen to that, thought Santiago.

They'd followed Tobias's wagon on over to the isolated corner of the hill where two other Mexican drovers lay and there lowered Jefferson Gonzales into the dry clay of an alien land. That time the big cook wept, and so did they all, except for Tobias, who gazed at the daylight moon. Santiago had led them through a prayer, and it was done. Purgatory had left the next day to help drive the stolen cattle back to the Sioux.

Bragg's legacy, thought Santiago. Or maybe it was the legacy of a frontier so hard to settle that it tore men's beliefs apart and made evil seem good, murder of Indians acceptable, willful conduct unrestrained by law or ethics desirable. He'd ponder that some winter's night with his feet propped on the grille of the stove. All that Bragg had left came down to nothing.

Eight. He turned wearily into the cellroom. He would take the girl out. His deputies would take the others.

Athena, wearing a new white dress, looked terrified.

"Do you want a minister?" Santiago asked once again.

"I don't believe in that stuff. Father didn't either."

"Do you have anything you need to say to lighten your soul? Any confession?"

"I'm a Bragg. My leg got broke, so shoot me."